It was the most dangerous face she'd ever seen.

A strong, chiseled chin darkened with stubble. Steely eyes narrowed against the morning sunlight. A forehead dusted with dark hair tousled from sleep. Though older, tougher, leaner, this was the same man who had fueled many of Andi's high school fantasies.

Donovan managed a quick smile, which had her heart leaping to her throat. "Your brother said we met once, though I'm afraid I don't remember. I'm Donovan Lassiter."

"Andrea Brady." She stuck out her hand. "My friends call me Andi."

"We call her Mama," Andi's daughter, Taylor, added.

She certainly didn't look like anybody's mother. At least not any Donovan had known. She was tall and slender, with wide honey eyes and sculpted cheekbones a model would die for. She wore no makeup, yet her skin was as fine as porcelain. Her unpainted lips were perfectly formed. Made for kissing...

Dear Reader,

Happy New Year! And happy reading, too—starting with the wonderful Ruth Langan and *Return of the Prodigal Son,* the latest in her newest miniseries, THE LASSITER LAW. When this burned-out ex-agent comes home looking for some R and R, what he finds instead is a beautiful widow with irresistible children and a heart ready for love. *His* love.

This is also the month when we set out on a twelve-book adventure called ROMANCING THE CROWN. Linda Turner starts things off with *The Man Who Would Be King.* Return with her to the island kingdom of Montebello, where lives—and hearts—are about to be changed forever.

The rest of the month is terrific, too. Kylie Brant's CHARMED AND DANGEROUS concludes with *Hard To Tame,* Carla Cassidy continues THE DELANEY HEIRS with *To Wed and Protect,* Debra Cowan offers a hero who knows the heroine is *Still the One,* and Monica McLean tells us *The Nanny's Secret.* And, of course, we'll be back next month with six more of the best and most exciting romances around.

Enjoy!

Leslie Wainger

Leslie J. Wainger
Executive Senior Editor

Please address questions and book requests to:
Silhouette Reader Service
U.S.: 3010 Walden Ave., P.O. Box 1325, Buffalo, NY 14269
Canadian: P.O. Box 609, Fort Erie, Ont. L2A 5X3

Return of the Prodigal Son
RUTH LANGAN

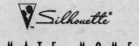
Silhouette®

INTIMATE MOMENTS™

Published by Silhouette Books

America's Publisher of Contemporary Romance

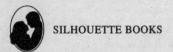

SILHOUETTE BOOKS

ISBN 0-373-27193-X

RETURN OF THE PRODIGAL SON

Visit Silhouette at www.eHarlequin.com

Printed in U.S.A.

RUTH LANGAN

is an award-winning and bestselling author. Her books have been finalists for the Romance Writers of America's RITA Award. Over the years, she has given dozens of print, radio and TV interviews, including some for *Good Morning America* and *CNN News,* and has been quoted in such diverse publications as the *The Wall Street Journal, Cosmopolitan* and the *Detroit Free Press.* Married to her childhood sweetheart, she has raised five children and lives in Michigan, the state where she was born and raised.

Dennis, this one's for you.
And for Tom, as well. With all my love.

Prologue

Chevy Chase, Md., 1981

"Bren. Call your brothers in before it gets dark."
Kieran Lassiter turned to his eight-year-old grand-
daughter, his voice still rough from the tears shed at
the funeral of his son. Police Sergeant Riordan Lassiter had been given a hero's farewell by the city of
Washington, D.C., after taking a bullet meant for his
partner. The day had been a long and emotionally
draining one for his widow, Kate, and her four children.

It was the first time any of the family had ever

seen Kieran Lassiter cry. This stern, bear of a man was a tough former cop who had become his family's anchor during this turbulent time. His daughter-in-law, Kate, the mother of his four grandchildren, was still reeling from her loss. But throughout the day she'd managed to keep her composure as she went through the motions of meeting and greeting the hundreds of officials who had turned out for the ceremony.

Now, at last, they had returned to their home in the nearby suburb of Chevy Chase, away from the pomp and grandeur, where they would be free to grieve in private.

Minutes later, as Kieran was pouring boiling water into a teapot, Bren returned, followed by two of her brothers.

Kieran looked up. "Where's Donovan?"

"Up in the tree house." Micah, the oldest at twelve, carefully hung his coat on a peg by the back door and tried not to stare at his father's coat, hanging on a peg beside his.

"Tell him to come inside." Kieran filled two steaming cups and handed one to Kate, who sat like a wilted flower at the big trestle table, her shoes kicked aside, her eyes red and swollen, though no one had seen her shedding her tears.

"He said he's never coming in." Five-year-old

Cameron missed the peg and left his coat on the floor until, seeing his grandfather's scowl, returned to the spot and carefully hung it beside Micah's.

Kieran glanced out at the gathering darkness. "Rain's turning to sleet again. Micah, climb up that ladder and make your brother come down this minute."

"Can't." Micah held his hands over the still-warm stove, rubbing them together while keeping his back to the others. He and Cameron had been shooting hoops to stave off the time when they would have to come inside and face the empty spot at the table. Now that they were home, their loss seemed all the more real. Everywhere they looked, they could see the evidence of the loving father they'd lost. "Donovan pulled the ladder up into the tree house so nobody could follow."

"He'll freeze to death up there." Kieran paced to the window, then back to the table, where Kate was already slipping into her shoes.

With a sigh she went to the back door and pulled on a coat before heading across the lawn, with the others trailing behind.

"Donovan." With her hands cupped to her mouth she shouted into the freezing rain.

A figure appeared at the entrance to the tree house. "I'm not coming down, Mom."

Kieran's tone was rough with frustration. "Stop giving your mother grief, boyo. She's had enough for one day. Now come down here. It's going below freezing tonight."

Donovan shook his head. "I have to be here. Don't you understand? Dad and I..." He stopped, swallowed, then struggled on. "Dad and I built this. It was our special place."

Kieran turned to Kate, expecting his daughter-in-law to put an end to this foolishness and order her son down without any further delay.

Instead she seemed to think about her son's words for several minutes before lifting her head. "All right." She passed a hand over her eyes and gave a soft shrug of her shoulders. "What do you need to get through the night?"

Kieran shot her a stunned look. His Irish brogue thickened with anger. "You'd leave a ten-year-old boy all alone in a tree house on a night like this?"

"I would. If it helped ease his pain." She wondered what would ease her own. She glanced up. "Tell us what you need, Donovan."

"Nothing. I don't need anyone or anything."

His reaction was so typical, she almost smiled. This, her middle son, had always been her most difficult child. The one to test her patience. The one to break the rules, or at least to push them to the outer limits. Riordan had called him his wild child. But he'd always said it with a trace of pride.

She turned toward her children. "Put a sleeping bag and some food in a bucket." She cupped her hands to her mouth. "Donovan, lower the rope you keep up there and we'll send you some supplies."

Bren went in search of a sleeping bag. Cameron filled a pillowcase with the things a five-year-old considered necessary for survival. Peanut butter. Cheese. Bologna. A slice of bread and a container of milk, and his favorite stuffed pig, that had been on his bed since he was an infant. He hated parting with it for even one night, but he figured Donovan needed it more tonight. He hoped his older brother would draw some comfort from it.

When everything was ready, Donovan lowered a rope, and Kieran grudgingly tied it to the bucket.

Just as it began to lift slowly off the ground, Micah shouted, "Wait." He raced out the back door and placed something on top of the pile, then called, "Okay. Take it up."

In the doorway of the tree house, they could make out the shadow of Donovan as he pulled the bucket inside, then lifted from the top of the pile the heavy pea coat his father had always worn so proudly. As he buried his face in it, he could still smell his father in the folds.

Micah glanced at his mother and saw her eyes, shiny with tears. "I hope you don't mind, Mom. I thought it might help Donovan."

There were no words. And so she merely nodded and pressed her cheek to his, surprised that her first-born was already as tall as a man.

As he watched his family return to the warmth of the house, Donovan Lassiter slumped down against the rough bark of the tree house, wishing he could cry. But the grief was too deep for tears. And so he sat throughout the long frigid night, with the scent of his father wrapped around him, his heart so badly shattered he feared it would never heal.

Chapter 1

Donovan Lassiter looked up from his computer and swore when the phone rang, breaking his concentration. Whoever was calling would just have to talk to his machine. He was in no mood for pleasant conversation.

"Donovan? Champ Mackenzie here. I know you're there. Pick up the phone."

Donovan was startled by the voice from his past. He and Champion Mackenzie had been college roommates. They hadn't seen each other for more than ten years.

He pushed away from his desk and began rummaging around the room in search of his phone. Still muttering, he tossed aside a towel, a shirt and three stray socks, before finding his phone, tucked into a box of books.

"Champ? How'd you find me?"

"You're not the only one with Washington sources, old buddy. It wasn't easy, but I called in a few markers and found out where you were holed up. I'm at a gas station in Prattsville. I'm coming up."

Donovan gave a sigh and ran a hand through his hair. "Now's not a good time, Champ."

"I don't give a rat's…" The voice paused, then said, "I'm coming up, Donovan. I need to talk to you."

Something in his tone had Donovan relenting. "When you turn off the highway, it'll look like nothing but a dirt path. Take the path to the left and you'll come to a gravel drive. Follow that up the hill and you'll see my place back in the woods."

"I'll be there in five."

"It'll take you more like fifteen. I'll be waiting." Donovan hung up the phone and made his way to the kitchen. The coffee he'd made himself at dawn was now the consistency of mud. He tossed it down the drain and started a fresh pot, then hunted through the cupboard for a clean cup.

When he heard the sound of his old friend's car,

he walked to the door and stepped out onto the porch.

His former roommate had put on weight, but Donovan recognized him instantly as he stepped from the car and made his way up the steps. He found himself grinning. "You wear your success well, Champ. Congratulations. A millionaire by the age of thirty."

"Didn't I tell you I would?" Champion Mackenzie grabbed Donovan by the shoulders and studied him. "What's with the beard and ponytail? You afraid somebody might recognize you?"

Donovan laughed and touched a hand to the shaggy dark beard that covered his chin. "I'd forgotten about this." He led the way inside. "I've been meaning to shave."

Champ paused on the threshold and stared around at the boxes littering the floor. "Just like you've been meaning to unpack one of these days?"

"It comes from years of living out of a duffel." Donovan shoved aside a stack of newspapers and made room on the sofa. "I've only been here a couple of weeks."

"A month, according to my sources. But who's counting?" Champ remained standing while he looked toward the computer on the desk by the window. "I heard you'd left the C.I.A. and were holed up in the hills writing a book."

"I've left government service." As always, Donovan refused to acknowledge what that service had been. The things he'd done, the secrets he'd uncovered for the past ten years, would go to the grave with him.

He started toward the kitchen, with his friend following. "A publisher has shown some interest in my proposed book about international crime and the way governments deal with it." He filled two cups and handed one to Champ. "Something tells me you didn't go to all the trouble of finding me and coming up here just to talk about my book." He gave his old friend a steady look. "Are you in some kind of trouble?"

Champ sipped his coffee before shaking his head. "Not me. My sister. I don't know if you remember Andi."

Donovan sat down at the table and stretched out his long legs, vaguely seeing in his mind a dark-haired high-school girl who had dropped by the dorm on a quick visit with friends. "If I did, I've forgotten. What's the trouble?"

"Her husband, Adam Brady, was killed in a plane crash along with his partner, Neil Summerville. It went down off the Maryland shore after taking off from National. The authorities suspected foul play but couldn't prove it. There wasn't enough of the plane or its occupants to make a case. Not long after that, the bank and business records revealed that Adam had systematically defrauded dozens of wealthy clients in a pyramid stock deal that went sour.''

Donovan crossed his arms over his chest. "Greed. The driving force behind most crime, whether it's the plain, old, garden-variety theft, or international theft on a grand scale. It's always greed." He looked up. "So what do you want from me?"

"I knew my brother-in-law, Donovan. I'd have trusted him with my fortune."

"So did a lot of other people, apparently."

Champion shook his head. "He wasn't a criminal. I know it. My sister knows it. But I want the rest of the world to know it, too. I want you to clear his good name."

"What makes you think I can?"

Champ smiled. "I know...we both know that you have the kind of contacts that can give you access to information that the rest of us mortals can only dream of."

There was no answering smile. "Why is this so important?"

"Because Andi has two little kids whose hearts

are broken. For their sake, I want their father's good name back.''

He saw a look come into his old friend's eyes. A look he'd seen so many times through the years.

Donovan stood up and walked to the window, staring at the wooded hills that he hoped would bring him the solace that had eluded him for so long. ''You know what buttons to push, don't you, Champ?''

''Yeah. Sorry. I'm desperate. I love Andi and the kids so much, I'd do anything for them.''

Donovan turned back, arms over his chest, deep in thought.

Champion studied this man who had once been his closest friend. It hadn't been an easy friendship. Donovan Lassiter held everyone at arm's length. Even his own family. It was as though the brutal loss of his father at an early age had made him afraid to trust anyone.

He'd aged in the years since college. His body toughened by years of work abroad; his face even more angular. The look of deep pain was still there in those midnight-blue Lassiter eyes. In fact, it seemed even more pronounced.

Donovan gave him a hard, steady look. ''What happens if I find out that Andi's husband was, in fact, a thief?''

Champ's voice deepened. "Then she and the kids will have to live with it."

Donovan continued to study him a moment longer. "I'll want access to all the information you have. You'll hold nothing back."

"It's yours." Champ took a step toward him and held out his hand. "I'll owe you big time."

"We'll talk about it after I've had a look at the facts. Maybe I'll ask for your firstborn in payment."

Surprised at the unexpected humor, Champion gave a grunt of laughter.

As they walked to the door, Champ suddenly turned. "Who owns that house down the hill?"

"I do. It came with the package."

"Is there anybody living in it?"

Donovan shook his head. "I haven't bothered to contact a Realtor yet, but I figure I'll rent it out when I need money."

"Name your price and I'll write you a check now."

It was Donovan's turn to be surprised. "You want to live up here in the hills?"

"Not me. My sister and her kids. Her son's having a bad time of it at school. He's being taunted by his classmates. Been in a lot of fights lately. Andi says his grades have gone from good to failing. I think a chance to get away over their summer break might be just what he needs. What they all need.''

Donovan thought about it a moment before nodding. "Okay. As long as they understand that my place is off-limits.''

His old friend gave another lingering look at the clutter of boxes. "Don't worry. I'll warn them that some crazy old bearded recluse lives up on the hill. They'll give you a wide berth.''

He whipped out a checkbook and signed it. "Fill in any amount you want.''

Donovan grinned. "Must be nice.''

"It is. You ought to try it. You know there's always a place in my company for you.''

"Thanks, my friend. But no thanks. We both know I'm not company material.''

As Champion turned away he had another thought and paused. "I ran into your brother Micah the other day. He seemed to think you were still out of the country.''

Donovan flushed. "I...haven't had time to let my family know I'm back.''

"Yeah. Well, make time. Before they hear it from somebody else.''

Donovan nodded. "I guess you're right.''

"One more thing.'' Champ tugged on his friend's ponytail. "You might want to consider a shave and a haircut before you head down to civilization. I don't think the Lassiter family is ready for a glimpse of the wild mountain man you've become, my friend.''

"Hi, Pop." Cameron Lassiter slammed into the kitchen and unceremoniously dropped his attaché case on the kitchen table, along with his jacket and tie.

His grandfather, stirring something on the stove, shot him a look that had him backing up to retrieve everything. Though he was now a successful lawyer living in a bachelor apartment above the garage, his grandfather still had the ability to make him feel like a careless boy.

He stood, juggling the coat and tie in one hand, the briefcase in the other. "What's for dinner?"

"Spaghetti and meat sauce. And salad, if someone—'' Kieran Lassiter swiveled his head, giving him that famous meaningful glance "—is willing to help make it."

"I guess I could. Just let me get rid of all this." Cam walked away, returning minutes later with the sleeves of his white shirt rolled above the elbows. As he opened the refrigerator and began assembling the salad fixings, he nodded over his shoulder.

"We're eating in the dining room tonight? What's the occasion?"

"Micah and Pru are coming." Kieran smiled at the mere mention of his eldest grandson and his new bride. With her sweetness and calm demeanor, she'd become a welcome addition to their large and rowdy family. "I thought it'd be nice to eat in the big room."

"How about Bren?"

Kieran smiled. "She just called and said she'd be right over. Her committee meeting up on the Hill was postponed."

Cam shook his head as he tore lettuce and sliced big garden beefsteak tomatoes into a salad bowl. "It's still hard to believe my bossy sister is a congresswoman."

"So it is." Kieran paused in his work. Smiled. "Though I'm not surprised. Our Mary Brendan was always in the thick of every debate in this house."

"She always got the best of you, Pop."

The old man's smile faded. "She was just a wee girl. She had a way of tugging at my heart."

"And didn't she know it." Cam was still chuckling when the object of their discussion came bustling in, dropping her briefcase on the big trestle table. Cam waited a beat, knowing it was only a matter of time before their grandfather shot her that familiar look.

He wasn't disappointed.

"Sorry, Pop." She snatched up her case and brushed a kiss over the old man's cheek as she hurried to the other room. Minutes later she was back, her suit jacket gone, her sleeves pushed over her elbows, ready to join in the kitchen chores just as Micah and his bride, Prudence, arrived, arm in arm.

Cam barely paused in his work while muttering, "It's the lovebirds. Can't you two keep your hands off each other for even a minute?"

"I detect a note of jealousy, little bro." Micah gave him a friendly punch in the arm as he opened the refrigerator door and peered inside.

"Are you looking for something to do?" Kieran smiled at his grandson's bride as she brushed a kiss over his weathered cheek.

"I was hoping Bren and Cam were doing enough for all of us." Micah helped himself to a slice of cheese from a plate.

"There's garlic bread to be heated, and a bottle of wine chilling that will need to be opened."

Micah reached for the wine. "Now this is something I can handle."

Pru began arranging garlic toast on a cookie sheet before setting it in the oven. Though she'd been in the family mere weeks, she fitted in as comfortably as though she'd been a Lassiter for a lifetime.

"Ah." Kate Lassiter breezed through the back doorway and immediately kicked off her sensible pumps, holding them in one hand while balancing her briefcase in the other. "Now this is a scene that more than makes up for the day's frustration."

"Tough day, Mom?" Bren paused to accept her mother's quick kiss.

"I've had better." Kate sighed as she breathed in the perfume of her father-in-law's spaghetti sauce. "But I think I'm about to let it all slip away."

"Maybe this'll help." Micah handed her a stem glass of tart red wine.

She sipped, sighed and smiled as she looked around at her family. Just then, out of the corner of her eye, she caught sight of someone sprinting up the back steps. A tall, lean man in faded chinos and a crew-neck sweater the color of oatmeal. There was no denying the athletic grace, like a sleek Irish wolf-hound, that defined her middle son.

For the space of a heartbeat Kate couldn't find her voice. Then she set aside her glass and flew across the room and into his arms.

"Donovan. Oh, Donovan. Is it really you?" She gave him a hard, fierce hug, before holding him a little away to study him more closely. Then she promptly burst into tears.

For a moment nobody spoke. Then all the chores were forgotten as his family gathered around for a noisy welcome.

"Oh, I've missed you." Bren was laughing as she wrapped her arms around Donovan's neck.

"That goes double." He swung his sister around and around before releasing her.

As he did, Micah slapped him on the back, before grabbing him close. "Why didn't you tell us you were home?"

"I'm home."

Micah roared with laughter. "Thanks for nothing."

"Gee, big brother." Cameron stood back and stared with a look of mock surprise. "Home at last? Somehow I expected you to look a bit less like an aging hippie and more like James Bond. After all, any respectable spy worth his pay should at least be able to afford a haircut."

"Careful, sonny boy." Donovan gingerly touched a hand to the shaggy hair that brushed his collar. "I'll have you know I just came from the barber. He cut off enough to make a couple of expensive wigs." With a wicked grin he lifted his youngest brother off his feet in a bone-jarring hug. When he stepped a little away, he gave him a long, slow appraisal. "You've done some growing up since I last saw you. When did you get to be as tall as me?"

"I stopped growing about ten years ago, bro. You should have stuck around."

"Yeah. You're right." Seeing his mother standing to one side openly weeping, he gathered her against his chest. "Hey now. None of that."

Kate touched a fingertip to his cheek before wiping the back of her hand over her eyes. "These are happy tears."

"Okay. I guess that's allowed." He turned to Pru with a smile. "I take it you're the new addition to the family. Sorry we haven't met before this."

"I'm Prudence. I prefer Pru." She blushed prettily. "Micah's wife."

He offered a hand. "Nice to meet you, Pru." He turned to his older brother with an arched brow. "I don't know what she sees in you, but I'll give you points for having excellent taste."

Micah gave him a hard, quick punch in the shoulder and was surprised by the layer of muscle. When Donovan returned the punch, it nearly rocked him back on his heels.

Kieran stood to one side, watching in silence. While the others had rushed forward to offer a welcome, he'd hung back, needing a moment to digest the fact that his grandson was really here. "You'd better drop those fists if you know what's good for you. If it weren't for the fact that dinner is ready, I'd send you both out back to shoot hoops."

"You don't mean to say you still get away with that?" Donovan gave a snort of laughter.

"I do, boyo. And if you're not a little more respectful, you'll find out for yourself." Kieran turned toward the stove and began draining a heaping pot of pasta. "Now why don't we all head into the dining room. It looks like our little celebration just grew into something much bigger."

As they gathered around the dining room table, Donovan noted how the others settled into the places that had been theirs since childhood. Kieran at one end; Kate at the other. Bren and Cameron, the youngest, facing Micah on the other. The only change was the addition of Pru, seated beside her husband.

As Donovan drew up a chair beside Micah everyone joined hands while Kieran intoned the familiar blessing.

"Bless this food and this family. Not only those of us gathered here, but those who can be here only in spirit. Bless especially our Donovan, who has been missing for so long and has finally been returned to us. And as always, bless Riordan, who watches over us all."

Donovan saw his mother wipe fresh tears before picking up her napkin. Then he was forced to field a hundred questions as he disposed of a mountain of spaghetti drenched in his grandfather's famous sauce.

At last he sat back, sipping his wine. "You'll never know how many times I've dreamed about this, Pop. Nobody makes pasta like you."

The old man beamed with unexpected pleasure.

"So." Kate sipped her tea and studied her middle son. Even after a fine meal and friendly conversation, surrounded by loving family, he didn't appear to be at ease. Instead, she could sense a tension in him. A subtle drawing away. "When did you get back, Donovan?"

He stared into his glass. "I've been back for nearly a month."

"A...month?" Kate nearly spilled her tea before carefully setting the cup on the saucer. "And you never called?"

"Sorry." He looked up, and the darkness was back in his eyes. "I had a lot of things to deal with."

"Are you leaving again soon?" Kate struggled to keep her tone even. The last thing she wanted was to sound as though she were whining, but the truth was she dreaded the thought of saying goodbye.

Each time Donovan went away, he took a piece of her heart with him.

He shook his head. "I'm out of…government service for good. I bought a house in the hills of Maryland."

"You bought a house?" Kieran's tone sharpened. "And you didn't think to tell any of us until now?"

Donovan met the older man's eyes. "I need to be alone for a while, Pop, while I sort out my life."

"It seems to me you've had plenty of time for that, boyo. More than—" Kieran saw Kate shake her head and bit back the rest of what he'd been about to say.

"I know you don't understand, Pop. In fact, I don't understand it, either." Donovan looked at his mother and saw the light going out of her smile. It hurt, knowing he was the one who always seemed to bring the darkness with him. "I may have found my niche. I'm writing a book on international criminals, and the loopholes in our laws that allow them to flourish." He gave a mirthless laugh. "I consider myself something of an expert on that."

"Is that what you were doing for the C.I.A.?"

Cameron saw the sudden frown on Donovan's face before he managed to compose himself. "My work for the government is over. Now I'm going to take some time just for myself."

"I'm glad." Kate picked up her cup and drank, feeling her nerves begin to steady. "Can you support yourself by writing?"

Donovan shrugged. "That remains to be seen. I've already had an offer from a publisher. And I got a healthy settlement when I left government service. I'll be fine."

"I know you will." His mother drained her cup and glanced at Kieran, who was studying his grandson through narrowed eyes. "What's for dessert?"

Kieran pulled himself back from the million questions that begged to be asked. "Brownies and ice cream."

"I'll get it, Pop." Before his grandfather could move, Donovan was striding out of the room, grateful for the chance to escape.

In the kitchen he paused beside the big bay window to stare at the battered basketball hoop above the garage. Minutes later he returned to the dining room with a tray of brownies and bowls of chocolate cookie dough ice cream.

When he'd passed them around and remained standing, Kieran looked up in surprise. "Aren't you having any?"

Donovan shook his head. "I need to work off my food. I think I'll shoot some hoops."

"I'll join you." Micah pushed away from the table, his sweet tooth forgotten.

"Me, too." Cameron wasn't about to be left out.

"I'm in." Not to be outdone by her brothers, Bren trailed after them.

Half an hour later, his mother and grandfather joined Pru at the kitchen window to watch as the four siblings did what they'd been doing since childhood.

As Donovan ruthlessly pushed and shoved and broke free to score yet another basket, it occurred to Kate that her middle son was still fighting his demons, as well as fighting for his place in the family. Though he showed a stoic face to the world, and used whatever bullying tactics he needed to stay competitive, the weight of his loss was apparent to anyone who bothered to look beneath the surface.

The tragedy of his father's death at the hands of a gunman was still the motivating force behind everything he did. Grief still weighed heavily on his heart.

Perhaps, she realized, it always would.

Chapter 2

It was dark when Donovan returned to his home in the hills. He liked the darkness. Was comfortable with it. He found he did some of his best work while the rest of the world was sleeping. And though he'd put in a full day, driving down to his mother's home and back, he wasn't feeling tired. In fact, the visit with his family had been just the stimulation he needed to spend a few pleasant hours at his computer. He was looking forward to it as he passed the rental house at the bottom of the hill.

The windows glowed with light. Behind the drawn curtains he could see movement.

He hadn't realized Champion's sister and family

had planned to move in so soon. Still, Champ had said they were coming up as soon as school closed for the summer.

He caught sight of a van parked beside the small shed at the rear of the house. The thought of people living so near had him frowning. He'd begun to enjoy the solitude of these hills. To savor the slower pace. There was no traffic. No horns. No brakes squealing. No peeling of tires. Best of all, no ambulance and police sirens breaking the night silence. Those were sounds guaranteed to wake him from a sound sleep and have him pacing the floor for hours in a cold sweat. There had been too many times that he, or one of his co-workers, had been rushed from the scene of carnage to a safe house if there had been no American hospital nearby.

As he parked and made his way up the steps of his porch, he glanced at the thick file folder lying by the door. Apparently Champ had stopped by after helping his sister move and, finding him gone, had left it on the porch, knowing nobody but Donovan would bother with it. One more reason to bless this backwoods lifestyle he'd recently adopted.

He stared at the documents with a frown, wondering again why he'd agreed to take on somebody else's problem. He'd told himself, when he left government work behind, that he'd concentrate on his own life for a change.

He thought of his younger brother's remark about James Bond. Was that how his family and friends saw him? If only it had been so. There had been nothing glamorous about the work he'd done. It had been dirty and dangerous, and there had been dozens of times when he'd thought about tossing in the towel and returning home to a nine-to-five job. But whenever he tried to picture himself with a wife and kids and a comfortable life in the suburbs, he knew he was fooling himself. From the time he'd been very young, there had been a devil inside, forcing him to push the boundaries.

The work he'd chosen had suited him perfectly. Until he'd had his fill. Now it was time to move on and find out what he wanted to do with the rest of his life.

The rest of his life.

How many times had he wondered if he would be around another day to utter such a phrase?

He let himself into the darkened house and snapped on the lights. After climbing over a row of tumbled boxes, he tossed aside his keys and started a pot of fresh coffee before sitting down at his desk and opening the folder. Within a few minutes, his plan to work on his book was forgotten. The computer remained off as Donovan lost himself in the bizarre details of the investigation of Adam Brady and his apparent slide into criminal behavior.

Though he'd been accused of bilking his clients out of millions, none of the money had been found. Authorities were investigating every angle, from the suggestion that he'd been leading a double life, and had stashed the money with a lover, to the possibility that his current wife knew where the money was hidden and was waiting until the heat was off so she could go about spending it.

The one thing everyone seemed to agree on was that Adam Brady had been guilty as sin. And only his death had saved him from an ugly trial and eventual prison time.

By the time Donovan fell into bed at dawn, he was inclined to agree with the authorities who were convinced of Brady's guilt. What other explanation could there be for the loss of millions of dollars?

Still, he had promised his old friend he would do his best. If he could find even one tiny flaw in the case, he would pursue it to its logical conclusion. At least then he would have the satisfaction of having done all that was humanly possible before closing the file on this dead man.

It was laughter that woke him. A child's high-pitched giggles that seemed to come from somewhere nearby.

Donovan pulled the covers over his head and tried to block the sound. It came again, louder and closer, until it seemed to be just outside his window.

He sat up, tossing aside the covers as he climbed out of bed and stalked across the room. He looked out the window, hoping to spot the culprit. When he saw two figures race around the corner of his house, he pulled on a pair of faded jeans and hurried, barefoot, to the door.

"Ohhh, Cory. Don't touch him. He might bite." A little girl was standing slightly behind a boy who was crouched down, reaching into the bushes.

There was a rustling sound and the boy jumped back, knocking the girl to the ground. As he turned to help her up, a fat woodchuck waddled deeper into the brush and disappeared from sight.

"He got away." Annoyed, the boy was about to start after the animal when he caught sight of Donovan and froze.

The little girl ducked behind the boy, peering fearfully around his shoulder. While his hair was dark, the girl's hair was pale wheat. Both of them had round, solemn faces and wide, honey-colored eyes. Even without an introduction, it was obvious they were brother and sister.

The boy's chin came up like a prizefighter, anticipating the punch. "We didn't mean to."

"Mean to what?" Donovan's eyes flashed fire. He halted a few steps away when he saw the fear in the little girl's eyes.

"Set foot on your property. Uncle Champ said we shouldn't. But Taylor saw the guinea pig and we thought we could catch it."

"That wasn't a guinea pig."

"It wasn't?"

Donovan shook his head, his anger quickly dissolving into mere annoyance. "It was a woodchuck. And he wouldn't like being caught." He glanced at the little girl, still hiding behind the boy's back. "Your sister was right. He'd probably bite if he felt cornered. Most animals will fight back if they have no other choice."

Because his hands had automatically closed into fists, he tucked them into his back pockets and decided to start over. "My name's Donovan. What's yours?"

The boy paused a beat, as though debating the wisdom of revealing his identity. It occurred to Donovan that even at this young age, the boy had already learned a painful lesson about the pitfalls of bearing a famous, or in his case, infamous name. How many times had he been teased and taunted about his father's crimes since the media had begun its attack?

"I'm Cory. And this is my sister, Taylor."

"Hi, Cory. Taylor." If Donovan couldn't manage a smile, at least he tried to appear less threatening. "How old are you?"

The little girl ducked her head and stared hard at the ground.

"She's five. And I'm nine." Cory pinned Donovan with a look. "You going to tell our mom we were on your property?"

"I don't think that'll be necessary."

Cory started to relax until Donovan added, "I think she's just found out for herself."

The boy kicked at a stone and muttered under his breath as a dark-haired woman came rushing toward them, looking completely flustered. Her cheeks were red, her breathing labored, as though she'd been running at top speed.

"Cory. Taylor. I told you to stay close to the house."

"We saw a guinea pig, Mom." The little girl forgot her fear now that her mother was near. "We almost caught it. But it got away. And our neighbor says it isn't a guinea pig. It's a woodpecker."

"Not a woodpecker." Cory's frown deepened. "A woodchuck."

"Oh, yeah." The girl smiled broadly. "A woodchuck. It would have bited us if we caught it."

"Bitten." Her mother automatically corrected her before looking at the man.

When she did, she felt something similar to an electric current sizzle through her. He was naked to the waist, wearing nothing but a pair of faded denims that looked as though they'd seen better days. He seemed not the least bit bothered by his lack of clothing. Dark hair matted his chest and disappeared beneath the unsnapped waistband of his jeans. His shoulders were wide, and corded with muscles. She moved her gaze upward to a face that had her heart beating overtime. It was the most dangerous face she'd ever seen. A strong, chiseled chin darkened with stubble. Steely eyes narrowed against the morning sunlight. A wide forehead, dusted with dark hair that was tousled from sleep. The only thing that softened his look was that poet's mouth, which at the moment was pursed as he regarded her. Though older, tougher and leaner, this was the same man that had fueled many of her high-school fantasies after a single glimpse.

"I'm really sorry. I warned the children not to come up here and bother you. And my brother warned them, too."

"No harm done." Donovan managed a rare,

quick smile, which had her heart leaping to her throat. "Champ said we met once, though I'm afraid I don't remember. I'm Donovan Lassiter."

"Andrea Brady." She stuck out her hand. "My friends call me Andi."

"We call her mama," little Taylor added.

She certainly didn't look like anybody's mother. At least not any Donovan had known. She was tall and slender as a reed, with short, dark hair that curled softly around a strikingly beautiful face. She had wide, honey eyes and high, sculpted cheekbones that a model would die for. She wore absolutely no makeup, yet her skin was as fine as porcelain. Her unpainted lips were wide and perfectly formed. Made for kissing.

The thought jolted him. If he hadn't been awake before, he was now.

"Nice to meet you, Andi. I see where Taylor and Cory get their eyes."

Her lashes lowered and she seemed eager to escape this man's direct stare. "I was unpacking and I thought I'd let my children get acquainted with their new surroundings. I never dreamed they'd come this far."

She turned to her son. "I expected you to see to your sister."

"That's what I was doing."

At his defiant tone she struggled to soften her own. "Okay. No harm done. Let's go." She started to put an arm around her son's shoulders, but he backed away as though repelled by her touch.

To cover the awkward moment she caught her daughter's hand. "Come on now. We'll leave Mr. Lassiter alone."

"But what about our woodchuck?"

"He isn't your woodchuck, Taylor. Remember what Mr. Lassiter said. If you manage to catch him, he could bite." She looked up suddenly. "Could he carry rabies?"

Donovan shrugged. "He's a wild creature. Anything's possible."

"What if we set out a cage?" Cory could see his little sister's lower lip quivering. Even though he was already tired of the game, he knew that she'd had her heart set on a pet. "We could lure him in with food."

Andi shook her head. "He isn't like a guinea pig, that has never lived anywhere but a cage. You heard what our neighbor said. This is a wild creature, Cory. He's used to being free. He belongs in the woods. Besides, Taylor can't have pets. Remember her allergies. Now say goodbye to Mr. Lassiter."

"It's Donovan." He was doing his best to be

pleasant. Not an easy task on a couple of hours sleep. He was as eager for this to end as she was.

"All right. Say goodbye to Donovan." Andi was already starting away, her daughter's hand firmly in hers.

The little girl glanced at Donovan, then, like her mother, lowered her lashes and stared hard at the ground as she struggled to keep up with the impatient strides.

When Andi realized that her son wasn't following, she turned. "Cory. Come with us."

"Why?" He held back, hands on his hips.

"You can give me a hand unpacking."

"Sounds like a lot of fun." The boy dug his hands in his pockets and trailed behind, calling glumly, "'Bye, Donovan. Sorry about—" he shrugged "—you know."

"It's okay. See you." Donovan stayed where he was, watching until they rounded the bend in the road.

As a lifetime member of a loud and overbearing family, he considered himself something of an expert on family dynamics. This was a family that was hurting. It was obvious that the little girl was so shy she tried to be invisible. Cory was a wounded, angry rebel, ready to break all the rules he could. Donovan had to smile at that. He'd know a thing or two about being a rebel.

Then there was their mother.

As he made his way back to the house, Donovan thought about Andi Brady. For someone so young, she had her hands full. A dead husband with a checkered past, a ton of unwanted notoriety and a couple of troubled kids. He'd bet any amount of money that her friends were probably avoiding her and her creditors were circling around, ready to jump in at their first opportunity to clear their own debt at her expense.

Still, she wasn't at all what he'd been expecting. He didn't know how he'd missed her the first time around, when he'd been in college and she in high school. A man would have to be blind not to notice a woman like that.

It would seem that Champion Mackenzie's little sister had definitely grown up.

"Here, Cory." Andi began unpacking a box of clothing. "I'll put your clothes on the bed and you can hang them in your closet."

He leaned against the wall, arms crossed over his chest. His look, as always lately, was one of defiance. "Why can't you hang them?"

"Because it's your closet. You may as well arrange them the way you'd like."

Andi turned away and began hauling out shirts, jeans and assorted jackets and sweats. As she worked she thought about what Champ had told her. He'd managed to persuade Donovan to look into Adam's case. Though her own hope had begun to fade, she had to keep trying, for the sake of her children. Champ had said that if anyone could find a needle in a haystack it was Donovan Lassiter.

Donovan Lassiter. She went very still, her work forgotten.

The first time she'd met him, in her brother's dorm, she'd been completely tongue-tied. Champ had warned her about his roommate, and had filled her in on the family history. While her girlfriends had flirted shamelessly, she'd hung back, too afraid to even speak to him. Like all teenage girls she found the solemn, moody Donovan a romantic figure. She'd even begun to weave a few fantasies about him. In her mind's eye, she saw herself bringing a smile to those angry lips and a gleam in those steely blue eyes. But once she immersed herself in college life, Donovan Lassiter had faded into a pleasant, romantic memory. Though she'd never completely forgotten him, she'd been startled by the intense feelings evoked by their little encounter just now. She'd felt that same impact when she'd looked into his eyes. And the touch of him had left her almost paralyzed.

She turned to look out the window at his house on the hill. It was almost completely hidden in the woods that surrounded it. Somehow she thought that would suit Donovan Lassiter. From what her brother had told her, he hadn't changed much from that solitary, lonely young rebel. Still, she was determined to go along with whatever demands he made on her children. If she had to, she'd keep them locked inside the house all day. It was little enough price to pay for what he might do for them in return.

"Mom?"

Cory's voice broke through her thoughts.

"You've folded and unfolded that sweatshirt a dozen times now. Want me to stash it in a drawer?"

"Oh." She managed a weak smile. "Here."

As she handed it over, she picked up the empty box, tucking it under her arm. "I think I'll start on Taylor's room now."

Cory didn't answer. He was holding a wallet-size photo of his father that had fallen to the floor. On his face was a look of pain mingled with anger.

She felt a knife twist in her heart. It was one thing to lose a father in a tragic accident. That would be enough to shatter a child's heart. But to discover that their father wasn't the hero they'd always admired, but a criminal who had stolen millions of dollars from unsuspecting victims, was a burden that no child should have to bear.

She let herself out of her son's room and closed the door before leaning against it and closing her eyes. Cory wasn't alone in his confusion. She'd loved Adam Brady from the first time she'd met him. She missed him so much she ached. And she had steadfastly refused to believe that he was capable of criminal behavior.

Still, sometimes in the stillness of the night, she found herself questioning everything. Her blind defense of a man who wasn't here to defend himself. Her gut feeling that he'd been a good, honest man. She'd even begun questioning their love. Had there been someone else? Could he have stolen millions and left them with a lover?

It was too incredible to consider, even for a moment. She hadn't imagined Adam's love or his goodness. Those who believed otherwise were wrong.

She took in a deep breath and started toward her daughter's room. There was no time to give in to self-pity. This was what life had handed her. Like it or not, she'd live with it.

Chapter 3

Donovan's day had slowly gone from bad to worse. Because he'd been unable to get back to sleep, he'd decided to begin his own investigation on the Adam Brady case.

At first glance, it seemed simple enough. Brady had been invited to join Neil Summerville in his fledgling investment company. Since Brady came from an old banking family, he was able to use his connections to secure some impressive accounts, and the two men had made millions for their clients, as well as for themselves. Though neither man was flamboyant, they lived well. Membership in one of the city's most exclusive country clubs. Homes that were showplaces in the rolling Virginia countryside. Their children attended prestigious private schools.

According to the documents filed by the district attorney, the authorities were already closing in on Brady and Summerville when their plane went down. It was then that an examination of their books showed that the only clients that had been defrauded were those handled by Adam Brady. In the beginning, the amounts of money funneled from the accounts had been small enough that the clients didn't notice. But then the thief had become bolder, helping himself to more and more of his client's funds, and covering himself by showing losses in various investments. It was only after one very astute client had caught the error, and complained to Brady personally, that the authorities had been notified. Brady had agreed to cooperate fully by opening his company books to an independent audit.

And then the plane crash.

Donovan flipped through the pages to the crash report. The plane and pilot had been leased through a small, reputable company located at Washington's National Airport. A flight plan had been filed with the proper authorities. The plan had been to fly to Chicago for a meeting with clients and to return the same day. The weather had been stormy, with high winds, but the pilot had been confident that once they flew above the storm, they would have no trouble. The plane had barely been airborne when it crashed off the Maryland shore. Recovery from water is always messy. This was no exception. Despite their best efforts, only parts of the plane and bodies were recovered. But from what was salvaged, the authorities could find no sign of foul play and ruled the crash an accident.

Donovan sighed and tossed aside the documents.

He shouldn't have taken this on. He had a book to write. A life to sort through. The last thing he needed was a greedy investment counselor and his grieving family messing with his mind.

He decided to walk down the hill for his mail. It was nearly a mile from his house to the main highway, where the mail was delivered. He liked it that way. It was one more thing that didn't intrude on his solitude.

After rummaging through a box for a clean T-shirt, he had to hunt up his shoes. He found one by the door, the other beside his bed. He picked his way between boxes and stepped out onto the porch, surprised to see that it was already late afternoon.

As he started along the path between towering evergreens, a fat woodchuck sat up and watched from behind a screen of ferns.

Seeing him, Donovan frowned. ''Hiding out from

those city kids, aren't you?'' He shook his head. ''I don't blame you. They don't know enough to leave wild things alone.''

The woodchuck waddled away, leaving the ferns rustling. As he continued along the gravel path, it occurred to Donovan that he could have been talking about himself as well. He was comfortable alone. Always had been. He resented the intrusion of other people into his life. That's why his government career had been such a perfect fit. Not only was he not expected to make permanent attachments, but it was actually frowned upon. A man with a wife and children was a liability. The most effective men in his work were, like him, loners, with nothing to lose except their own lives. As for being wild, it went with the territory. There had been no timid men in his line of work. At least none who'd survived.

He caught sight of the rental house up ahead and lifted his head at the smell of woodsmoke. Since it was too warm for a fire in the fireplace, it must mean they were having a cookout. He stuck his hands in the pockets of his jeans and noticed that the front porch had been swept and the cobwebs removed from the overhang. Not that it mattered. Though he owned the house, he didn't care what they did with it. As far as he was concerned, it was theirs as long as they paid the rent.

He followed the rough road to the highway and paused at the row of mailboxes. After retrieving his mail he started back along the same trail. He hadn't taken more than a couple of steps before he felt the hair at the back of his neck begin to prickle. He paused to tie his shoe. As he did, he chanced a quick glance around. Though there was no one in sight, he was certain he was being watched. It was second nature to Donovan to always trust his instincts.

Tucking his mail in his back pocket he continued walking, all the while listening for any sound that seemed out of place. Gradually he sorted it out. A soft footfall in the woods to his left. Definitely not an animal. He slowed his pace, and realized that the footsteps slowed, as well. When he picked up the pace, he could hear the footsteps moving faster.

When he reached a spot where the trees grew together, forming an arch that blotted out the light, he took a quick turn into the woods, pausing beside the trunk of a tree. Within moments he saw a shadow approaching. In one smooth motion he reached out and closed his hand around a skinny wrist.

Cory Brady let out a yelp and looked as though he'd just seen a ghost. "Hey. What're you doing?"

"I might ask you the same thing. Anyone sneaking up on me could find himself in a whole lot of trouble." He released the boy's wrist and noted the quick flare of challenge in Cory's eyes. "Something in particular you wanted to know about me? Or were you just having fun?"

"How'd you know I was here?" Cory rubbed his flesh and wondered at this man's strength. The boy's arm felt as though it had been caught in a steel trap.

"Maybe I have eyes in the back of my head."

"Only moms have that."

"Yeah." Donovan nodded. "Now that you mention it, I seem to remember my own mom seeing all the things I was hoping she wouldn't."

The boy stepped back, putting some distance between himself and this mysterious man. "How'd you know I was there?"

Donovan shrugged. "I have my own personal radar. Why were you following me?"

It was the boy's turn to shrug. He looked down at the ground and kicked at a stone. "Sorry. I just…" He glanced up, then away. "Uncle Champ said you were a secret agent or something."

"More like or something." Donovan stepped back on the path and started walking. "So, you wanted to see if I was passing secrets to some foreign courier?"

"Maybe." Cory moved along beside him and gave him a nervous glance. "Were you?"

"Sorry to disappoint you. I was picking up my

mail.'' As they neared the house, Donovan motioned toward it. "How's your new place?"

"It's all right. Mom's going nuts trying to get everything cleaned up and put away. She can't stand clutter."

"Yeah?" Donovan almost smiled. "She'd really go nuts at my place. I've been there a month and still haven't unpacked."

"You mean it?" Cory was clearly impressed. "And nobody yells at you or anything?"

"There's nobody to yell. I live alone."

"Yeah. That's what Uncle Champ said. I mean…" The boy looked embarrassed. "He said you like being alone. And Taylor and I weren't supposed to bother you."

Just then a worried voice sounded from the back yard. "Cory."

"That's Mom."

Donovan nodded. "I can tell."

"She's always bugging me to let her know where I am. Even when I'm just going for a walk."

"You're new here. She's probably afraid you'll get lost."

"She yelled at me back at our other place, too. She's been scared ever since…" His words fell off and he gave a quiet hiss of breath.

"Maybe you ought to let her know you're all right."

"I will. It's just—" he kicked at the dirt "—I just like to be left alone sometimes, you know?"

"Yeah. I know the feeling."

The front door slammed and Andi Brady cupped her hands to her mouth to shout, "Cory!"

She was startled to see him standing with Donovan. "Oh, thank goodness. I was worried."

The boy's tone hardened. "I told you not to worry about me."

"I try. But I just can't help myself." She smiled as she walked closer. "If I'd known you were with Mr. Lassiter, it would have put my mind at ease."

"Don't you remember? He said we could call him Donovan."

"Sorry. I forgot." She glanced at Donovan. "We were just going to eat. Will you join us?"

As he began to shake his head in refusal, she added quickly, "Nothing fancy. Just hot dogs on the grill in the backyard. We're eating on the picnic table, because we haven't unpacked the kitchen boxes yet."

Cory's mouth turned down in a frown. "I said I'd do it tomorrow."

Andi touched a hand to his arm. Just a touch, but he jerked away as though burned.

She sighed. "I'm not trying to lay blame, Cory. I know you said you'd do it tomorrow. For now the outdoor grill is just fine."

She turned to Donovan, struggling to keep her smile in place, though it was an effort. "Want to join us?"

He tried to remember if he'd eaten all day. The only thing he could recall was an apple. And that had been hours ago. But more important than the offer of food was the fact that Andi Brady was wearing a pair of shorts that displayed her long, long legs, and a shirt tied at the midriff. He'd have paid an admission fee just to sit and stare. "Okay. As long as you're sure it's no trouble."

Cory brightened. "We've got plenty of hot dogs. We bought a whole package in that little store in town when we drove up here last night."

Andi nodded her agreement. "You two go around back and I'll be right out. I have some potato salad in the fridge."

Cory led the way up the driveway and around to the back of the house. Andi had covered the old wooden picnic table with a colorful red-and-white cloth, and had cleverly set the paper plates and napkins in a clear plastic case with flatware on top to keep them from blowing away. She'd filled a crock with ice and cans of soda.

"You want a soda?" Cory popped the top from a can and took a long drink.

"Thanks." Donovan did the same before looking around. Though the Brady family had only been here a day, it already looked different. When he'd had a tour of the house before buying the property, it had looked tired and a bit worn. Now, with curtains at the windows, and the back porch as clean as the front, the house seemed to have a festive air. Especially with the wonderful aroma coming from the grill. It had Donovan's mouth watering.

"Here we are." Andi stepped out on the porch carrying a round serving bowl.

"I'll take that." Donovan was across the lawn in quick strides.

By the time she set foot on the bottom step, he was reaching out to take the bowl from her hands. As he did, Andi felt the quick flash of heat when their fingers brushed.

Knowing her cheeks were burning, she turned away, muttering, "I'll get the mustard and ketchup."

"I have them, Mom."

Andi nearly ran over little Taylor in her haste to escape.

"Thanks, honey." She took them from her daughter's hands and carried them to the table, grateful for the few moments to settle her nerves. "Well. Looks like we have everything we need." She tucked a stray curl behind her ear and busied herself at the grill.

Minutes later she passed around a plate of hot dogs in buns. "Help yourselves to the potato salad."

Seeing Taylor struggle to open her soda can, Donovan held out his hand. "I'll do that."

The little girl lowered her gaze until she seemed to be watching him through her lashes. It was something her mother did, too, and he found it oddly endearing.

"Here you go." He popped the top and handed it back.

"What do you say to Donovan, Taylor?" Andi stood with her hands on her hips.

"Thank you, Donovan."

"You're welcome."

"Daddy always did that for me."

Out of the corner of his eye Donovan saw Cory's quick frown. "Yeah. Dads are good at that. And for lifting heavy things."

"He used to lift me onto his shoulders at Cory's soccer games so I could see over the crowd."

Donovan gave her a smile before turning to Cory. "You play soccer?"

"Not anymore."

"You decided you didn't like it?"

"Yeah." The boy busied himself drowning his hot dog in ketchup and relish.

Though he didn't elaborate, Donovan thought there might be more to it than just giving up on the sport. Recalling what Champ had said about his nephew, he found himself wondering if some of the team members had given the boy a hard time about his father. It could be the reason for the silent treatment.

He absently took a taste of potato salad and looked up in surprise. "This is good."

Andi's cheeks turned almost as red as her daughter's. "Thanks. It's one of those things I love making in the summer."

"And one of the things I love eating." He helped himself to more.

Andi touched a napkin to the dab of mustard on her daughter's chin. "Are there any places of interest I might want to show the children while we're here?"

"Depends." He picked up his soda. Drank. "If you're looking for history, there's plenty around. You can tour the battlefields, either alone or with a group. Plenty of historic homes, as well. Personally, I tend to ignore the tourist things and concentrate on simpler things."

No surprise there, Andi thought. This wasn't a man who would mix with a busload of tourists, unless there was a compelling reason.

Aloud she merely said, "Like what?"

He shrugged. "These woods are full of surprises. Deer. Raccoons." He winked at Taylor. "Woodchucks and woodpeckers."

Despite her shyness, the little girl giggled behind her hand.

Andi looked unconvinced. "Couldn't we get lost?"

He grinned. "It's a possibility. But before you start out, you fix a few landmarks in your mind. My place, up on the hill, would be a good one. Or a particular rock formation or tall tree. Then you note where it is in location to where you're headed." He glanced across the table. "I think Cory could probably be trusted to take a few treks into the woods without getting himself lost."

The boy shot him a grateful look.

"I don't know." Andi rubbed at a spot on her temple, where the beginning of a headache was making itself felt. This move to a strange place, and the stress of unpacking, had added to her tension. "I don't think I'm ready to let Cory go off by himself in a place he's never been before."

"There you go again." The boy exploded with

anger, pushing aside his plate as he leaped to his feet. "Why can't you trust me with anything?"

"I do trust you, Cory." Andi's own meal was forgotten. "It's just that I don't know what I'd do if you didn't make it home. We have no family here. No friends to turn to."

"I'd rather be someplace where nobody knows us than to be surrounded by friends who call us names." He started toward the back porch.

Andi got to her feet. "You didn't eat a thing, Cory."

"I'm not hungry." The boy stomped up the steps and let the back door slam behind him.

In the silence that followed Andi turned to Donovan, her cheeks flaming. "He wasn't always like that. It's just since—"

She looked defeated, and Donovan realized she was struggling to hold herself together. Little Taylor studied her mother with a mixture of sadness and fear.

To distract the little girl, Donovan pointed to a spot at their feet, where a colony of ants was attacking some crumbs that had fallen from her plate. "Will you look at that."

When Donovan knelt down, the little girl squatted beside him.

He pointed. "Those are the worker ants. It's their

job to haul those giant crumbs down long tunnels to their warehouse.''

"They have a warehouse?" She looked up at him with those big eyes that could melt glaciers.

"That's right. And lots of different places for all of them to eat and sleep. Every one of them has a job to do. Some are probably already breaking down those crumbs into food for everyone.''

"The way Mama does for me?"

He nodded. "And some are still hauling the heaviest of the loads.''

"I bet those are the daddies."

He smiled his agreement. "And then there are some down there unpacking from their last home.''

He could see Taylor trying to decide if he was serious or having fun with her. When she glanced up at her mother and saw that the smile had returned to her eye, she dimpled. "You're teasing, aren't you, Donovan?''

He winked. "I can see that you're a very smart little lady.''

"I'm not a lady. I'm a little girl."

"Well then, I guess I'll have to call you a lady in training. How's that?''

Taylor thought about it a moment, then giggled. "Mama, am I a lady in training?''

"Yes, you are." Andi was surprised at how quickly her headache had faded.

Just watching her daughter relax in Donovan's company had made all the difference. For these few moments Taylor had forgotten her extreme shyness around strangers. For that Andi was grateful.

Now if only someone would work a miracle on her son, as well.

Donovan pointed to the table. "Taylor, why don't you gather up the paper plates, and I'll carry in the rest."

Andi was on her feet at once. "There's no need. I can take care of this."

Donovan touched a hand to her shoulder. "You did the cooking and the setting up. Sit here and enjoy the sunset. Taylor and I will have this cleaned up in no time."

Andi sank back down on the wooden bench and watched as Donovan charmed her little girl. Within minutes he and Taylor disappeared inside. When they returned, Taylor was giggling.

Andi's head came up. "What's so funny?"

"Donovan said you won't have to wash the potato salad bowl, Mama."

"You mean he already cleaned it?"

"Uh-huh." Taylor giggled harder. "He licked it clean."

Donovan gave her a look of mock anger. "You promised not to tell."

"I couldn't help it." She put a hand to her mouth to stifle more giggles.

"I guess I'll know what to make if you ever agree to come to dinner again." Andi got to her feet and drew her daughter back against her, wrapping her arms around her as she did.

"I'm a sucker for potato salad. And that was the best I've ever eaten." Donovan looked into two pairs of honey-colored eyes, and felt a strange stirring. "Thanks for having me to dinner."

"You're welcome. I hope you'll come back again." Andi nudged her daughter. "Don't you want to say goodbye to Donovan?"

"'Bye," Taylor called.

"Good night, ladies. Or should I say lady and lady in training?"

As he walked away, Donovan heard the trilling of laughter carried on the soft summer breeze.

It was, he realized, one of the most pleasant sounds he'd heard in these woods since he'd moved in. In fact, this entire evening had been surprisingly pleasant. With nothing more than a hot dog on the grill and a can of soda, he'd had a grand time, thanks to the Brady family.

They were an interesting mix. Cory was hurting.

No doubt about it. That defiance was all a cover for the pain.

Donovan cringed. He ought to know. He'd spent a lifetime masking his pain the same way.

As for Taylor, she may be painfully shy, but once she warmed to strangers, she was just fine.

So was her mother. It was obvious that Andi was feeling the strain of coping with life alone. She'd looked so sad and lost when Cory lashed out at her, Donovan had wanted, more than anything, to wrap his arms around her and tell her that it would be all right.

Not a good idea, he realized. He was going to be investigating her husband's business practices and poking into dark places that could cause this family even more pain. The last thing he needed to do was to get personally involved.

Still, when he'd briefly touched her while taking that bowl from her hands, he'd felt a sizzle through his entire nervous system.

He chuckled in the darkness. He'd definitely been away from civilization too long. Put one pretty female in front of him and his hormones went into overdrive.

What he needed, to get Andi Brady out of his mind, was a long bout at the computer, delving into the workings of the mind of the international criminal.

Chapter 4

Donovan stared at the computer screen and absently picked up the cup beside his keyboard. He was surprised that the coffee was cold. Hadn't he just poured it a few minutes ago? Or had it been more than an hour ago?

He glanced at the window, amazed to see that it was already daylight. How was it possible that the night had slipped away so soon? Apparently, he'd been more absorbed in his work than he'd realized.

Before he could return his attention to the monitor, he caught sight of a blur of movement near the edge of the woods.

Standing, he pressed a hand to the back of his

neck as he strolled to the window for a better look. He recognized Cory, sporting a denim jacket and a backpack, just stepping into a stand of evergreens. The sight of the boy had Donovan smiling. It looked as though Cory had managed to persuade his mother to give him some space after all.

Stretching, Donovan made his way to the bathroom. A long hot shower was just the ticket to ease his cramped muscles. He shaved, then stripped and stepped under the warm spray. A short time later he stood over a box of clothes, debating whether to dress for the day or try a few hours of sleep. He decided the day was simply too inviting to be wasted in sleep. He pulled on clean denims and a light-blue T-shirt and reminded himself that he would soon have to consider doing a load of laundry. But not today.

He walked barefoot to the kitchen to see if he had any food left in the refrigerator. The last banana had turned black, and he tossed it into the garbage. That left a single apple. He polished it on his pant leg as he walked from the room.

A knock on the door had him hurrying to open it. Andi was standing on the porch with little Taylor behind her.

"Well. Good morning. Come in." As Donovan stood aside, he caught the look on Andi's face when she spotted the boxes littering the floor. "I've been…ah…meaning to unpack one of these days."

"Yes, well…" She knew she was staring, but she couldn't seem to tear her gaze from the mess. There were boxes everywhere. Clothing tossed over every inch of furniture, and even scattered about on the floor. There were cartons of books spilling over tabletops, desktops, shelves. There were bags, boxes and canisters crammed with photographs. There were storage shelves littered with binoculars, cameras and electronic gadgets of every kind.

"I'm sorry to bother you, Donovan, but I'm worried sick about Cory. He was gone when I woke up. He left me this." She held out her hand. In it was a slip of folded paper.

Donovan unfolded it and read, then glanced at her. "What's the problem? It says he's going for a walk."

"At dawn?" Her voice trembled. "He knew I'd forbid him to go. That's why he left before I was awake. But that doesn't excuse him. Donovan, Cory doesn't know anything about this area. He thinks he's all grown up, but he's only nine. If anything happened to him…"

"Hey, now."

He closed his hands over her upper arms and squeezed gently. As he had the previous night, he felt the sizzle of heat that caught him by surprise before he quickly lowered his hands to his sides. Touching Andi Brady was definitely dangerous. He'd have to remember that in the future.

"I saw Cory going into the woods less than an hour ago. Why don't you let me go after him?"

"He has an hour head start on you. He could be anywhere by now."

"An hour's not a problem. A day or two might be cause for alarm, but an hour's just a walk in the park. I'll find him."

Something in the way he said it had her looking at him more closely. The things her brother had speculated about Donovan Lassiter's secretive work came rushing back. She had visions of a man being dropped by parachute at night into a foreign country and left to survive by his wits alone. At this moment she could almost believe such things about him. "You...won't tell him I sent you?"

"Not even a hint. Cory isn't the only one who feels like exploring the woods. He can't blame me if I happen to run into him, can he?"

Seeing that she wasn't convinced, he touched a hand to hers. Just a touch, but the heat was there, as strong as ever. This time he was prepared for the punch. "Go home, Andi. I'll find him."

She took a deep breath and caught Taylor's hand as she headed out the door.

As she walked down the steps Donovan called, "Andi?"

She turned.

"I know you feel that he's testing your patience, and he is. But he's also testing himself. So relax. He'll be just fine."

She nodded before turning away. But the worried look on her face told him she wasn't convinced.

With a camera strapped around his neck, Donovan stepped into the coolness of the woods and took a moment to get his bearings. Then he started walking. Anyone who saw him would think he was admiring the new spring growth as he stopped to study the pale-green ferns, and noted beside them the footprints heading south. A short time later he paused to touch the bough of a stately pine, and removed a denim-blue thread that had been caught on the bark. When he came to a stream he followed along the banks until he reached the top of a steep drop-off. The water tumbled nearly a hundred feet to a pool far below, surrounded by more evergreens.

Donovan spotted Cory sitting on a rock, his knees drawn up, his look pensive.

Taking the camera from around his neck, he made

his way down the steep hill, pausing every few feet to snap a shot of the waterfall, the pool, the surrounding countryside.

Finally as he approached the rock where Cory was seated, he lowered his camera. "Hey. I see you found my favorite spot."

"This is yours?" The boy scrambled down and stood facing him. The hands at his sides had automatically fisted.

"Not really. I guess it belongs to whoever owns this piece of land. But it's a great place to sit and think."

"Yeah." Cory sank down in the grass, relieved that he wasn't in trouble from trespassing. "Do you come here a lot?"

"Not often. I do most of my thinking at my computer. But when I really need to get away, this is the place."

Cory nodded toward the camera. "That's pretty slick."

"You want to see it?" Without waiting for a reply Donovan handed it over.

Cory carefully examined it. He peered through the viewfinder, switching from wide-angle to close-up, then flipping a switch that turned it into an infrared night viewer. When he looked up, his eyes were wide. "Wow. This is really cool. It must have cost a fortune."

Donovan shrugged. "Government issue. They made it a parting gift to me."

When Cory started to hand it back, Donovan shook his head. "If you'd like to try a few pictures, go ahead."

"You mean it?"

Donovan nodded. "If you stand on that rock, you ought to be able to get the entire waterfall and pond in the shot."

The boy did as he suggested and clicked off a shot. Then, for good measure, he took a second one before climbing down.

He handed back the camera. "You on your way to somewhere special?"

"No. Just thought I'd walk a bit. How about you?"

"I guess I'd like to walk a bit, too." Cory brushed hair from his eyes and fell into step beside him, unwilling to admit that he was feeling more than a little relieved for the company. The size of the forest had been overwhelming.

As they moved deeper into the woods Donovan touched a hand to the boy's arm and pointed in silence. A herd of deer came walking toward them, pausing every so often to nibble the tender green leaves of evergreens. Cory and Donovan stood perfectly still, hardly daring to breathe until the herd slipped away.

"That was awesome." Cory turned to Donovan. "Why didn't you take a picture?"

"The sound might have spooked them."

"Oh. Yeah." The boy was clearly impressed by what he'd seen.

They walked on, picking their way over fallen logs, pausing to study tiny jewel-like violets and miniature star-shaped blossoms as white as snow.

Donovan nudged the ground with the toe of his hiking boot. "Looks like that owl I hear outside my window every night enjoyed a midnight snack right here."

"How can you tell?"

"By what he left behind." He picked up a small stick and stooped down, jabbing it into the lump of debris. "Look here. Fur. Tiny bones. These are the parts of the mole or mouse the owl can't digest. He spits them back out."

Cory looked at him with new respect. "How do you know so much?"

Donovan laughed. "It's called living. If you live long enough, you're bound to pick up some information along the way."

"I don't know. I don't think my mom would ever know anything about owls."

"Maybe she would. If she wanted to be a scientist or naturalist or a veterinarian."

"Is that what you wanted to be?"

"For a while." Donovan smiled, remembering. "But mostly I just wanted to be like my dad."

"What does he do?"

"He was a cop."

"Like the ones on those TV shows?"

Donovan nodded. "I suppose."

"Then why didn't you become a cop?"

"I guess I wanted more. More action. More adventure. More challenge."

Cory digested that for a moment before asking, "Does he like what you do?"

"My dad's dead. He was shot when I was ten."

That stopped Cory in his tracks. His voice shook when he finally found the courage to ask, "Did you get a chance to say goodbye to him?"

"No." Even now, after all these years, the shadow of pain was still there. "That was the worst thing for me. Not getting a chance to tell him what he meant to me."

"Yeah." Cory dug his hands in his pockets and stared hard at the ground. "My dad..." He sucked in a breath. "My dad left for the airport while I was still asleep. Later, my teacher called me out of class to tell me my uncle was on his way to pick me up. I thought maybe Dad had changed his mind and had decided to let me fly with him to Chicago. I could hardly wait for Uncle Champ to get there. Then, when he did, he gave me the news that Dad's plane…''

In the silence Donovan closed a hand over the boy's shoulder. Squeezed.

Cory looked up, his eyes dry. ''Some people are saying bad things about my dad.'' The boy's tone lowered. ''There were reporters standing all over our driveway, in our yard, peeking into windows, snapping pictures. One even stuck a microphone in my little sister's face.''

Donovan thought about the very public funeral of his own father. He'd blinked back tears until his eyes had burned like fire. But he'd managed to hold it all inside until he was alone.

''And then the kids at school started.'' A look of fire came into Cory's eyes. ''The first time I came home with a bloody lip, I couldn't tell Mom why. I could have told my dad. He'd have understood. But moms just don't get it.''

''Yeah.'' Donovan could think of nothing comforting to say. His own father had been heralded as a hero. How could he possibly offer comfort to a boy whose father was being accused of stealing millions from helpless victims? What was worse, Donovan was halfway convinced of it himself. The district attorney had made a very strong case against Adam Brady. "Is that the reason you dropped off the soccer team?"

Cory kicked at a log. "Who needs it?"

"Didn't any of your friends stick by you?"

"One. Billy Watson. But after he went home with a black eye, his mom said he couldn't hang around with me anymore. She told him I was a bad influence."

"That's tough."

Cory shrugged. "It doesn't matter. I'm glad Uncle Champ found this place. Nobody here knows our name."

"You can't hide out forever."

The boy turned bleak eyes to Donovan. "Who says?"

"The world's too small, Cory. Sooner or later you'll run into someone who recognizes you. Someone who knows about your father. Then what will you do?"

The fire was back. The small hands fisted at his sides. "Just let somebody try to say something about my dad. I'll make them sorry."

Donovan chuckled.

"What's so funny?"

"I just realized that you remind me of somebody."

"Who?"

Donovan sighed. "A kid I knew. He was so mad at the world after his father died, he wanted to strike out at anybody and everybody. Even his own family."

"Did he?"

"Yeah. Way too often."

"What was his name?"

"Donovan Lassiter."

Cory stood perfectly still, watching as Donovan moved ahead. Then he started running until he'd caught up with him.

They walked in silence until Donovan handed the boy his camera. "Take a look through the viewfinder at the top of that tree. What do you see?"

Cory did as he was told and gave a gasp. "It looks like a hawk."

"Yeah. That's what I figure. When he's ready to fly, snap off a couple of shots."

The two remained silent for several minutes until the bird spread its wings. Cory took picture after picture as the hawk began to fly, then to soar.

When it disappeared from sight, the boy handed

back the camera. "You've reached the end of that film."

"I'll have this developed and pick up some more." Donovan dropped the roll of film into his pocket before slipping the camera around his neck.

He glanced up at the sky. "I think it's time to head back."

The two hiked in silence for several miles.

Suddenly Cory pointed. "Now I know we're heading in the right direction. There's the roof of your house in the distance."

"Good going, Cory. That's a good landmark to keep in mind, since it's high enough to see even with all the trees around."

The boy felt a quick sense of pride at his words.

When they emerged from the woods, the sun had already made its arc across the western sky.

Donovan paused on the gravel path. "Your mom will be glad to see you."

Cory shrugged. "I guess. You want to walk home with me?"

Donovan could see that the boy didn't want to face his mother alone. "I suppose I could."

Cory brightened. "Thanks for letting me use your camera."

"You're welcome. I'll bring you the snapshots if any of them turn out."

"That'd be neat." He was smiling as he danced up the steps of the back porch and shouted, "Mom, I'm home."

"Cory." Andi was beaming with pleasure as she looked up from stirring something on the stove. Seeing her son's smile she resisted the urge to rush across the room and hug him, afraid it would only make him frown.

She was wearing a simple black tank top and jeans that showed off her slender frame to its best advantage. Just the sight of her had Donovan forgetting the long, hot miles he'd hiked all day.

Taylor came dashing into the room, obviously pleased to see her big brother. "Mama made your favorite supper."

"Tacos?" The boy's smile deepened.

"Uh-huh. And carrot cake for dessert."

Cory turned to his mother. "Can Donovan stay?"

She nodded. "Of course he can."

Donovan was already shaking his head. "I can't impose on you again. I really have to go."

"You're not imposing." Andi brushed a damp curl from her eye. "I made enough. I'd really like you to stay for supper."

He inhaled the fragrance of spiced beef and chilis, and felt his stomach protest the fact that, as usual, he'd forgotten to eat. On top of that was the fact that she was the prettiest thing he'd seen all day.

He gave her a heart-stopping smile. "Okay. You talked me into it."

"Good." She added another place setting. "If you'd like to wash up, Cory will show you where."

As Donovan followed Cory from the room he turned in time to see Andi mouth the words *thank you.* He winked, then turned away.

Minutes later they were gathered around the kitchen table.

As Donovan filled his plate, Andi turned to her son. "I found something besides your note this morning, Cory. You must have been up half the night to get all those boxes unpacked, and everything arranged so neatly in the cupboards."

Around a mouthful of food he said, "I told you I'd do it."

"Yes, you did." She walked to where he sat and pressed a kiss to his forehead, much to his dismay. Ignoring his look of horror she remained beside him, a hand on his shoulder. "Thank you, Cory."

"You're welcome." He ducked his head. But Donovan saw the pleasure in his eyes.

Before the rest of them had taken more than a few bites, Cory managed to wolf down his supper and was helping himself to seconds. "We saw a

herd of deer in the woods. And a hawk.'' He emp-
tied his second glass of milk. ''And Donovan
showed me where an owl had dinner.''

''Sounds like the two of you had a grand adventure.''

''Yeah.'' While they finished their meal, Cory
went on to describe the waterfall and the pool nearly
hidden by tall rocks and evergreens. By the time
they had enjoyed slices of carrot cake, washed down
by tall glasses of milk, he had taken them through
every minute of his day. The contrast between his
behavior this day and the way he'd acted the previous day was amazing.

''Donovan let me use his camera. It's really
neat.'' Cory looked up at his mother. ''Isn't it something, that Donovan and I ran into each other in the
woods?''

Taylor glanced at her brother over the rim of her
glass of milk. ''Mama asked Donovan to find you.
She was worried.''

''What?'' For a moment Cory merely stared at
his little sister. Then, as the realization dawned, he
pushed away from the table and glared at his mother.
''You didn't trust me?''

''I...was worried, Cory. You've never been in
those woods before. I was afraid you'd get turned
around and—''

"I can't believe you did that. I told you..." He struggled to get the words out. "I told you I could take care of... Oh, what's the use?"

He gave her one last furious look before running out of the room and racing up the stairs. While the others watched and listened in silence, they could hear the slamming of his door as he closed himself in his bedroom.

Chapter 5

In the silence that followed, Taylor turned mournful eyes to her mother. "Why is Cory mad? Did I do something wrong?"

"Hush, darling." Andi rounded the table to drop a kiss on her daughter's cheek. "It wasn't your fault. It was mine."

She sighed, and Donovan could see the strained look return to her eyes. "I made coffee, Donovan. Would you like some?"

He was already on his feet, directing her back to her chair. "I'll get it. You look like you could use some, too."

When she nodded, he poured two cups of coffee. "Cream or sugar?"

"Just black." She accepted the cup from him and lifted it to her lips, hoping it would restore her flagging spirits.

Taylor wiped milk from her upper lip. "Did you and Cory see any bears, Donovan?"

"No bears." Donovan managed a smile. "If we had, you would have seen us home a lot sooner. But we did see deer."

"Were they reindeer?"

He shook his head. "And not an elf in sight, either. Just a few ordinary deer. But we had a good hike. I think, after the miles we put in today, Cory will sleep tonight."

At the mention of sleep the little girl yawned, and Andi said softly, "Would you like to go upstairs and get on your pajamas?"

Taylor nodded.

"Go ahead, then, honey." Her mother managed a smile. "I'll be up in a little while to tuck you in bed."

"Okay, Mama. G'night, Donovan."

He grinned. "Good night, Taylor."

When they were alone, Andi's smile faded. She looked across the table at Donovan. "He was so happy when he walked in. It's been a year since I've seen that light in his eyes. And it was wiped out in an instant because of me.''

''Stop beating yourself up, Andi.''

She gave a hard shake of her head. ''I let him down. Not once but twice. It's bad enough that I didn't trust him. But I made it worse by asking you to pretend your meeting was an accident. That's the same as lying.''

''You're a mother. Every mother worries about her children. But you've got an added burden, because you're alone and in a strange place.''

''That's no excuse for not trusting my son and then lying to him.'' She pushed away from the table. ''I'd better go upstairs and tuck Taylor in. I know she'll be fretting about her big brother. I swear they're connected at the hip. Every time he hurts, she bleeds for him.''

When she left the room, Donovan sat a moment, sipping his coffee, deep in thought. Then he got up and began to clear the table. By the time Andi returned, he had the dishes in the dishwasher and had wiped down the table and stove top.

She looked around in surprise. ''You didn't have to do this.''

''I wanted to.''

Despite her heavy heart she couldn't help laughing. "After seeing your place this morning, I wasn't sure you knew how to clean up."

He gave her one of his rare, heart-stopping smiles. "I admit I'm a little rusty. But I guess it's like riding a bike. You never forget." He held up the coffeepot. "Want a fresh cup?"

"Thanks." She leaned against the counter while he filled her cup and his own.

As he handed her the coffee he asked, "You feeling tired?"

She shook her head. "Just the opposite. That little scene with Cory has me wired. Why do you ask?"

"I'm sure Champ told you about our agreement."

She nodded.

"I thought it was time to ask you a few questions about your husband's business."

She sighed. "I figured sooner or later you'd ask."

"You can tell me to stop at any time. I don't want to cause you any further grief, Andi. But there are things I need to know."

She nodded. "All right, then. Would you like to sit in here or in the living room?"

"This is fine." He carried his cup to the table and sat facing her as she settled herself across from him. He had to remind himself not to think about those soft, honey eyes or that perfect mouth, and concentrate on business. It wouldn't be easy. She reminded him of a wounded bird. And he'd always had a soft spot in his heart for helpless creatures.

"How well did Adam know his partner, Neil Summerville?"

"They met in college, then lost contact until a few years ago, when they met at a dinner party in Washington. They talked for several hours, and when Adam admitted that he wasn't crazy about his job at the bank, Neil invited him to join his investment firm. Adam and I talked about it, and when I had no objections, Adam negotiated a very favorable deal that made him a full partner."

"What did Adam have to do in exchange for a partnership?"

"He agreed to use his connections to bring in wealthy clients. It's done all the time in big business."

Donovan nodded. "Besides the clients he would bring with him, there was the name. The reputation. Isn't that right?"

Andi smiled. "The Brady family prides itself on its reputation. Until Adam—" she stopped, tried again "—until now, there's never been even a hint of scandal surrounding their name."

"I imagine they're not too pleased with the notoriety."

Andi stared into her coffee. "That's putting it

mildly. They've closed ranks. Refused all interviews. But they've also shut us out.'' She sighed. ''I don't mind for myself. My brother has been great. Champ has been at my side from the first day. But my heart aches for my children. They haven't seen their grandparents since the funeral a year ago.''

''Adam's family is blaming you?''

She sighed again. ''They need someone to blame. And since their son is dead, they prefer to think that I probably hounded him to leave the family business and make more money somewhere else.'' She looked up and met Donovan's eyes. ''The truth is I knew Adam was unhappy in the family business. I just wanted his happiness. Money never entered into the equation.'' She shook her head. ''I guess my mother was right all those years ago.''

''Right about what?''

''She used to shake her head and call me her beautiful dreamer. I was the child who always believed in happy endings. And now look at my life.'' She fell silent, looking as though she might break down and cry at any moment.

To give her time to compose herself, Donovan stood up and crossed to the stove, returning with the coffeepot. After topping off their cups he returned to his seat at the table.

"Did you ever notice any sudden change in your husband's behavior? Something to indicate that he was unhappy with the way things were going at the new firm?"

She shook her head. "Oh, he and Neil had their differences. Neil was always at the office. He was the first one there in the morning, and the last one to leave at night. He would spend entire weekends working on his clients' portfolios, while Adam wanted his weekends free to be with me and the children. But their discussions never seemed as heated as the ones Adam had with his father and uncles, before leaving the banking business."

"So there was bad blood between Adam and his family when he left?"

"He was the heir apparent. When he left, they realized they would have to bring nonfamily members into positions that had once been held only by blood."

Donovan paused a moment, considering the enormity of his next question. "Could Adam have been angry enough with his family to want to do something that would hurt them?"

"Are you asking if Adam would steal from his own clients, just to bring shame to his family? The answer is emphatically no. Donovan, my husband was a good, decent, honorable man."

"And you believe in his innocence?"

She nodded and lowered her head, but not before he saw the shadow of doubt that flickered in her eyes.

He decided to change directions.

"Did he and Neil often fly together to client meetings?"

"Not often. Usually one of them would conduct the meeting, while the other would remain in town. But the meeting in Chicago was a luncheon for a group of potential clients who were bringing a great deal of money to the firm. Neil and Adam thought it best if they both attended."

"Did they usually lease a private jet?"

"Most of the time they used commercial carriers. But Cory had a soccer playoff. Adam told Neil that he needed to be home for it. So Neil arranged for a private plane that could get them back in plenty of time for the game."

"Neil made the arrangements?"

She nodded, before passing a hand over her eyes in a gesture of weariness.

At once Donovan was on his feet. "You need your rest. We can do this another time."

"No." As he started toward the back door she placed a hand on his sleeve. "It...it helps to talk. My family and friends avoided any mention of it, for fear of causing more pain. So many of my former friends turned away from me after the funeral...." She took in a long, deep breath. "I've gone over this so many times in my mind, looking for something, anything, that would restore Adam's good name. Especially for the sake of my children. Taylor's still too young to understand the implications. But Cory's so hurt. And I don't know how to reach him."

Donovan placed a hand over hers and struggled to ignore the rush of heat. But there was no denying what he felt each time they touched. "I can understand some of what he's going through. There's so much anger when the person you love is snatched away without warning. But Cory has the added burden of being forced to hear and read some pretty lousy things being said about his father. It isn't bad enough he has a hole in his heart that will never be filled, but now it's being rubbed raw with all that pain and anguish."

She took a step back. "Champ said you lost your father at about the same age."

He nodded.

Andi looked up hopefully. "When did you stop missing him?"

"I'll let you know when that happens."

At his words she understood the shadow of pain

that was always there whenever she looked into his eyes.

"Oh, Donovan." She instinctively reached a hand to his cheek. "I'm sorry. Here I am telling you about our troubles, when you're still dealing with your own."

At her tenderness he absorbed a blow to the heart and had to take in a quick breath. "It happened a long time ago, Andi."

"And it still hurts."

"Yeah." He looked down into her eyes and knew he had to kiss her. Walking away, right this minute, would have been the smart thing to do. But for Donovan, it wasn't even an option.

He reached out instinctively, drawing her close as he lowered his head, capturing her mouth with his. There was nothing soft or inviting about his kiss. In the space of a single heartbeat he drew her fully into it.

She thought about pulling back, but she was frozen to the spot. It was impossible to move.

Heat poured between them as they slipped deeper into the kiss.

He thought he'd been prepared for this. But as his mouth moved over hers, the sensations that ripped through him had him dragging her closer, until her body was imprinting itself on his. He longed to

touch her everywhere. But all he permitted himself
was the brush of his hand along her back. Even that
simple movement had him aching for more.

Andi absorbed the shock as his touch sent sparks
dancing along her spine. She'd known, of course,
that he was attracted to her. A woman could tell
those things. And the attraction was returned. What
woman wouldn't be attracted to a sexy, dangerous
man like Donovan Lassiter? But she hadn't thought
beyond the attraction. It had been too many years
since she'd flirted. As for kissing a man, there had
been no one except Adam from the day they'd become engaged. Now here she was, letting this man
kiss her. What shamed her even more was that she
was returning his kiss.

And what a kiss. It took all her willpower to keep
from wrapping her arms around his neck and beg-
ging for more. Still, she kept her arms firmly at her
sides, her hands clenched into tight fists to keep
from touching him.

What had she gotten herself into? She'd wanted
this. Wanted desperately to feel his mouth on hers.
And yet she was afraid. Afraid of where it might
lead. She wasn't ready for this. Especially with a
man like Donovan Lassiter.

He lingered over her mouth as long as he dared,
wishing he could take more. The thought of lying

with her, loving her, had his head spinning and his world tilting at a crazy angle.

He was playing with fire here. This wasn't a woman he could simply love and leave. Andi Brady was the kind of woman a man loved for a lifetime. She had responsibilities. Commitments. None of those things were even considerations in his life.

He gathered her so close against him she cried out. That had him lifting his head and staring down at her in stunned surprise.

His eyes narrowed as he rubbed his hands along the tops of her arms in a motion meant to soothe. "Sorry."

She wondered if he had any idea just what his touch was doing to her. It took her a moment to find her voice. "Apology accepted."

His smile was quick and dangerous. "I wasn't apologizing for the kiss. If I have the opportunity, I'll do it again."

"Is that—" she marveled that she could get any words out over a throat so constricted "—a promise or a threat?"

"Take it any way you want. I'm just giving you fair warning. But I didn't mean to be so rough." He ran his fingers lightly up and down her arms.

Andi couldn't control the shiver that raced up her

Return of the Prodigal Son

spine. If he kissed her again, she'd be completely lost.

She was relieved when he took a step back, breaking contact.

"I'd better go."

As he walked away she crossed her arms over her chest, struggling to hold herself together.

He put a hand on the door and turned. "Most folks up here don't lock their doors." He gave her a smoldering look that said more than words. "In your case, it might be wise to use the locks."

Andi stood where she was, listening to the sound of his footsteps on the gravel path.

When she was certain her legs would carry her, she walked to the back door and turned the lock. Not that it mattered, she thought. He looked like a man who wouldn't be stopped by a locked door.

She pressed her forehead to the cool glass and waited for her heart to return to its normal rhythm.

It shamed her to admit that she had been completely lost the moment his mouth touched hers. If he hadn't had the sense to put an end to that kiss, this night might have taken a very different turn.

Despite the heat of the summer night, she shivered as she made her way up the stairs to her bedroom. The thought of being loved by Donovan Lassiter was every bit as tempting now as it had been when she'd been a schoolgirl.

And every bit as foolish.

If his reputation was to be believed, Donovan didn't love; he simply took his pleasures, whenever, wherever he pleased. He plundered. He collected trophies. And then he moved on, never to be seen again.

She had no intention of being any man's conquest. In fact, she had no intention of being any man's anything, ever again. She had her hands full just getting through her days as a mother. She'd leave the fanciful romances to others.

She slipped into bed, determined to put all thought of Donovan Lassiter out of her mind.

Chapter 6

Donovan typed some words on his keyboard, initiated the search engine and sat back, watching as dozens of pages of information began flashing across the screen.

It had been three days since he'd seen Andi Brady or her children. He ought to be grateful for that little scene at her place. It had pushed him into an orgy of work to keep from thinking about her.

When he wasn't working on his book, or on the Adam Brady file, he was sleeping. The last time he'd crashed into bed, he'd slept for fourteen hours. At the moment he felt like a new man. Of course, he hadn't shaved for days. And there was no food in the house. But getting food would have required getting dressed, driving into town and shopping. None of which appealed to him. He much preferred to subsist on dry cereal, since he was out of milk, and peanut butter, eaten directly out of the jar, since he had no bread or crackers left to spread it on.

He was nearly out of clean clothes, as well. He would soon have to deal with dirty laundry. But not just yet. Today he was wearing a pair of khaki shorts that had been new ten years ago and a faded camp shirt he'd won in a poker game in Ghana from an old pal, Joe Bentley. He frowned, remembering the friend who had gone down in a helicopter over San Salvador. Too young. So many of them had died too young.

He glanced at the crash investigator's report and noted Adam Brady's age. Thirty-four. Another one gone too soon.

Donovan leaned back in his chair and closed his eyes. *Only the good die young.* It had been a favorite phrase among the group of brash young government agents who had called themselves The Lost. If the saying proved to be true, he could hope to live a very long life.

Suddenly something on the monitor caught his eye. He hit a button, stopped the scroll, and read through the page. Satisfied that this was what he'd been searching for, he printed it out and added it to the growing pile of documents on his desk.

The sound of voices had him strolling to the window.

Cory and Taylor were stalking something in the bushes. Donovan stepped out onto his front porch.

"There he is."

"Keep your voice down, Taylor." Cory was wearing his usual frown. "Mom'll skin us if we bother Donovan."

Donovan crept up behind them and said in his best whisper, "Not to mention what Donovan will do to you."

"Oh." Taylor gave a shriek and ducked behind her big brother, then peered out from behind him.

Cory lifted his chin as he faced Donovan. "We weren't being loud."

"That's right. You weren't. But why are you whispering?"

"Mom said we couldn't bother you."

Taylor's voice trembled. "Are we bothering you, Donovan?"

"No. I needed to take a break from my work. This is the perfect time to get some fresh air." He nodded toward the bushes. "You chasing that woodchuck again?"

"Uh-huh." Taylor was quick to defend herself.

"I don't want to put him in a cage. I just want to get close enough to give him some food."

"He's pretty good at getting his own. What did you want to feed him?"

Taylor held out her hand. In it were some carrot sticks. "Mama said he's probably a veginarian."

He tried not to laugh. "Vegetarian."

"Uh-huh." Taylor's smile grew. "But Cory said he probably eats bugs and stuff. What do you think, Donovan?"

"I think he eats both. Bugs and vegetables."

"If I sit right here in the grass and hold out a carrot, do you think he'll come up and take it from my hand?"

"I doubt it, honey." Donovan gave her a gentle smile. "He's a little bit shy. Do you know what that means?"

"He's shy?" Her eyes grew round, and he could see that she was feeling a real kinship toward the woodchuck.

"That's right. I think you'd have to leave the carrots here in the grass and walk away before he'd come up and help himself."

"Then I'll put them right here." She carefully arranged the carrots in a circle before stepping back.

"Cory. Taylor." Andi's voice drifted up from the gravel drive. When she rounded the bend and found her children with Donovan, two bright spots of color appeared on her cheeks.

"I'm sorry." The first sight of him was a shock. How could any man who hadn't shaved and was wearing a wrinkled shirt and shorts do such strange things to her heart? She knew men who wouldn't look that good if they were dressed in black tie. Yet here he was, barefoot and rumpled, making her blush like a schoolgirl. "Cory and Taylor, I told you not to bother Donovan."

"He said we aren't bothering him, Mama." Taylor caught her mother's hand and led her toward the tall grass. "Donovan says the woodchuck is shy, so I left him some carrots to eat when we're gone."

"That's nice, honey." Andi turned to Cory. "Time to go."

"Where?" Her son had his arms crossed over his chest, the way he did when he was ready to give her a hard time.

"Into town. I have to get some groceries and run some errands."

"I don't want to go."

"You have no choice. I'm going, and you can't stay alone."

"Why? I'm not a baby, Mom."

"I know you aren't." She tried to keep her tone light, but it wasn't easy. "I wouldn't be much of a mother if I didn't look out for your safety. So I guess you'll just have to come along with me while I run my errands, whether you like it or not.''

Donovan could see that Cory was about to dig in his heels and make a scene. ''Why don't you let him stay with me?''

The boy couldn't hide his surprise. ''You mean it?''

''Sure.''

''Can I stay, too?'' Taylor pulled away from her mother and hurried over to stand beside her brother.

''Now, Taylor...''

Before Andi could refuse, Donovan nodded. ''You can both stay. I'm thinking it's time I un-packed, anyway. You two can give me a hand. If you can stand the clutter, that is.''

''You're sure?'' Andi seemed torn between relief at not having to drag her reluctant children along and regret at leaving them in Donovan's pigsty.

''Yeah. We'll be fine.''

''Is there anything you need while I'm in town?''

''As long as you're offering...'' Donovan dug into his pockets and came up with a handful of money. ''I don't need much. Some milk, bread, eggs and fresh fruit.'' As he handed it over he caught a whiff of perfume. It seemed ironic that someone who looked as sweet and fresh and vibrant as a spring morning could smell so sinful.

"All right." As she accepted the money from his hand, she felt the heat of his gaze and stepped back, as though sensing she needed to get out of harm's way. "Well. I guess I'll see you later."

"Oh, wow." Cory's anger of the past few days was forgotten. "Come on, Donovan. Let's get started. You've got all that great junk."

"Yeah. May as well." Donovan stood a minute more, watching the sway of Andi's hips in the knit, ankle-hugging dress that flattered every line and curve of her body. She looked like a fashion model with those strappy sandals and that little sweater tossed carelessly over her shoulders. All she needed was one of those wide-brimmed hats to look as if she was going to a garden party.

He turned away, grateful for the distraction of the boy and girl. At least with them around he wouldn't have time to torment himself with thoughts of what he'd like to do with their mother.

"Where are you going to put all this stuff?" Cory was already attacking the first box.

"I've got those shelves and cabinets over there." Donovan pointed to the two wall units. "And there are more shelves in the kitchen and in my bedroom.''

''You've got a bedroom?'' Cory glanced at the sofa. ''I figured you slept there.''

''I do. Sometimes. But only when my bed is covered with too much stuff.''

Taylor looked up. ''Didn't your mama make you hang your clothes when you were little?''

He paused and smiled. ''Not only my mom, but my grandfather. Now there was a real nag.''

Cory paused. ''Did you see your grandfather a lot?''

''Every day. He lived with us.''

''Why?'' Cory dropped a handful of shirts and sat back on his heels.

''After my father died, Pop moved in with us. I think it was only going to be for a little while, until my mom could pull things together. But then she decided to go back to college and then law school, and he just stayed.''

''That's pretty neat.'' Cory began rummaging through another box, hoping to find more than dingy shirts and jeans. ''I think our grandparents are mad at us.''

''Now why do you say that?'' Donovan picked up the clothes scattered across the floor and sofa and began carrying them toward the laundry room.

Cory trailed behind. "'Cause we haven't seen them since our dad died."

"Maybe they're hurting."

The boy shook his head and bent to retrieve a sock that had fallen from Donovan's arms. "Mom let us call them a few times. Gramps always said Grandma couldn't come to the phone. She was busy or shopping or out with friends. But she never called back."

"How about your mom's parents?"

"Her mom is dead. And her dad lives in California with his new wife. He wanted us to come and stay with him for a while, but Mom said we belong here."

Donovan sorted the clothes into piles and started the washer. Then he led the way back to the front room, where Taylor was happily studying an assortment of masks she'd found in one of the boxes.

"Look at me, Cory," she called, holding a mask to her face.

"You look weird." He turned to Donovan. "Where'd you get those?"

"A village in Africa. They were a gift from the chief." He crossed the room. "Let's put them on this shelf, Taylor."

The little girl used a stool to reach the shelf, where she began arranging the masks in a row.

Cory walked over to help, studying the intricate design of the mask he pulled from a box. "Why did the chief want to give you a gift?"

"Because I helped him out with a little problem."

"What kind of problem?"

Donovan smiled, remembering. "I helped him end a little war." He stood back. "They look good there, Taylor. I think I'll hire you as my decorator."

The little girl giggled.

Cory moved to the next box and opened it to reveal a pair of high-powered binoculars. As he lifted them to his eyes and began fiddling with the dials, he let out a hoot of excitement. "Wow. I can see every feather on that bird up in that tree." He fiddled some more and then, unwilling to believe what he was seeing, held the glasses away, then back to his eyes. "Donovan, I can see the bird's eye. And the speckles on his feathers."

"Yeah. They're pretty powerful."

The boy ran to a window and continued peering at everything, amazed at what he could see through them. Soon he was distracted by Taylor's yelp of pleasure when she found, in another box, an assortment of pottery and baskets. "These are pretty, Donovan." She held up an intricately woven basket. "Can we put them on the shelves, too?"

"Sure, honey. You hand them to me and I'll put

them up here." He began arranging the baskets and pottery, then added a few of the bigger pots beside the fireplace. "How's this?"

"Pretty." She dimpled, enjoying her task as decorator.

Cory walked up beside him and knelt beside one of the baskets. "Where'd you get all this stuff?"

Donovan shrugged. "Here and there. Some of this is from Colombia, some from Guatemala." He chuckled as he fingered one of the pieces of pottery. "This is from Nigeria. An old woman handed it to me as I was getting on the plane and told me it had belonged to her mother."

"Why did she give it to you?"

"She wanted to thank me. For getting her son out of some trouble."

"Were you a policeman?" Taylor asked.

"In a way. Sort of a global policeman."

"Weren't you ever afraid?" Cory looked up from the box he was rummaging through.

Donovan sat back on his heels. "Sometimes. Everybody is afraid of something. Whether it's a fear of strangers or a fear of flying or a fear of snakes or spiders."

Taylor shivered. "I'm afraid of all those things."

"You're scared of everything," Cory scoffed. "Even your own shadow."

"Am not."

"Are, too."

She relented. "Maybe I am. But I can't help it."
She turned to Donovan. "What do you do when
you're scared?"

"If I have something important to do, I just put
aside my fear and deal with whatever comes my
way. Otherwise I'll let fear rule my life. Not only
rule it, but ruin it. And I just can't do that."

Taylor looked at him adoringly. "Are you
stronger than Superman?"

He chuckled. "Sorry. I'm not even close. But we
can all act like him when we're in trouble. And do
you know why?"

The two children, staring at him with rapt attention, shook their heads.

He touched a finger to his temple. "Because this
is where our strength lies. Our brain. If we think
things through and refuse to give in to our fears, we
can get through almost any dangerous situation."

Cory pulled out a ragged coat from the bottom of
a box and held it up. "Why would you keep something like this?"

Donovan looked over. Something flickered in his
eyes before he composed himself. "That was my
father's. Even though it's falling apart, I like wearing it." He took it from the boy's hands and hung

it almost reverently on a hook by the front door. Then he pointed toward the kitchen. "Come on. There are lots more boxes in there. Let's get to work."

After unloading her groceries at her house, Andi maneuvered her van up the gravel path toward Donovan's. She hadn't intended to be gone so long, but it had taken her a while to find the cleaners, the bank and the post office in a strange town. She figured by now Donovan was probably ready to tear out his hair trying to deal with Taylor and Cory and the million questions they were sure to pester him with. It couldn't be easy for a solitary man like him to have two little kids underfoot for hours.

She came to a stop and climbed out. The thought of what she'd bought had her smiling. He'd asked for only milk, bread, eggs and fruit. But when she'd opened her hand and found two crisp hundred-dollar bills, she couldn't resist buying him a few more staples.

She wondered if he knew how much he'd given her. Probably not. Maybe he thought he'd given her twenty-dollar bills instead of hundreds. At any rate, she had scrupulously accounted for every penny she'd spent.

She lifted a bag of groceries and started toward

the porch, expecting to see her children racing out to meet her. Instead, her knock was greeted with silence.

Puzzled, she opened the door and looked around in amazement. The boxes were gone. The litter had disappeared. The shelves, which had stood empty, were now arranged with an assortment of fascinating items.

She set the bag on a coffee table and noted idly that it had been polished to a high shine. In fact, the entire room had been transformed. Now that she could see the sofa, it looked new and very expensive. As were the two wing chairs on either side of the fireplace. The rug on the floor was Oriental and gorgeous. The candlesticks on the mantel appeared to be excellent crystal.

Hearing laughter from the back of the house, she made her way there and paused in the doorway of the kitchen. Donovan was folding clothes. Cory and Taylor were seated at the table eating something from bowls and using chopsticks.

Chopsticks?

"Mom." Cory looked up, obviously delighted. "Look. Donovan's teaching us to eat like he did in Beijing. These chopsticks belonged to the family he lived with there."

"Beijing?" She arched a brow. "You lived in China?"

"Just for a little while."

"He can speak Mandarin. And seven languages. Go ahead, Donovan. Say something in Portuguese."

"You speak...Portuguese?"

He shrugged. "Not very well. Just enough to get by."

Feeling slightly confused, Andi nodded toward the bowls. "I thought you were out of food."

"Pretty much. But I remembered that I had some rice, and Cory and Taylor wanted to try eating with chopsticks. Of course, if it were a true traditional meal, I'd have had to go dig up some grubs."

"Grubs?" Her eyes narrowed, and she wondered if he was having fun with her.

He set a pile of clean shirts to one side and touched a finger to her cheek. "You sound like a parrot. Did you bring food?"

"Food. Yes." She fought to ignore the thrill that streaked down her spine at his touch. What in the world was wrong with her? "It's out in my van."

"Good. I'll get it."

"I'll help." Cory was up like a flash.

"Me, too." Taylor wasn't about to be left behind.

While the three of them were gone, Andi took a moment to look around the sparkling kitchen. The dishes in the open cupboards appeared to be English bone china, and very beautiful. An open drawer revealed exquisite Irish linen cloths. The pottery on the counter had a definite South American flavor. And the elegant tea set was Oriental.

Donovan and the children returned, laughing and chatting as they began unloading the bags and stashing the food. It occurred to Andi that they seemed as easy and natural as though they'd always been doing this together.

Donovan held up a package of pasta. "Is this for me?"

Andi blushed slightly. "I just thought you might want more than milk, bread and eggs."

"But pasta requires cooking. And I only cook if I'm having company."

"I'm sorry. I just thought…"

Before she could finish Donovan winked at Cory and Taylor. "Looks like you're staying for supper." He filled a pottery bowl with fresh fruit and set it to one side of the counter before catching the look of surprise on Andi's face. "Oh. Sorry. You're invited too, of course."

"You…cook?"

He gave a rumble of laughter. "I'm a man of many talents, Mrs. Brady, of which cooking is but one." He nodded toward the doorway. "Now why don't you kids take your mother into the living room and show her what we managed to accomplish while she was off having fun in town.''

"Come on, Mom.'' Cory caught her hand, and Taylor took her other hand.

She dug in her heels. "But what can I do to help?''

"You can relax. Put your feet up. Take the rest of the day off, Mrs. Brady. The kids and I have everything under control.''

"Oh, wait.'' She dug into her pocket and handed him some money. "Your change.''

"Thanks.'' Without even glancing at it, he shoved it into his pocket while the two children led her from the room.

She was, she thought as she allowed herself to be directed toward the front room, feeling a little like Alice when she fell down the tunnel. Where in the world had she landed? Who were these laughing, happy aliens? And what had they done with her surly son and shy daughter?

Chapter 7

Donovan carried a tray into the front room, where Taylor was showing her mother the collection of masks.

"Donovan said I could set them on this shelf. Didn't I do a good job?"

"A very good job, honey."

"Donovan says I'm always going to be his decorator."

"I can see why." Andi turned when she caught sight of Donovan setting the tray on the coffee table. "Is everything all right?"

"Everything's perfect. I've got my pasta sauce simmering, and the salad chilling." He handed her a glass of red wine. "I think you'll like this. I picked it up in Spain a few months ago. They make some fabulous wines."

She sipped and nodded. "You're right. I love it."

"Good." He motioned toward the tray. "Soda for you two."

Cory and Taylor helped themselves to frosty glasses while Donovan poured himself some wine.

Taylor walked to the window. "Do you think the woodchuck ate the carrots, Donovan?"

He smiled. "Why don't you go outside and check."

"Will you come with me, Cory?"

The boy crossed to the door. "Sure." He turned to Donovan. "Can we take our soda with us?"

"I don't see why not."

As the two ran outside, Andi walked to the window to watch. When Donovan stepped up beside her she turned to him with a smile. "I can't believe what you've managed to accomplish in a matter of hours."

"You mean the clutter."

She shook her head. "I mean my children. I haven't seen them this relaxed in a year." She lowered her voice. "What kind of miracle worker are you?"

He tugged on a lock of her hair. "No miracles

here. We just had a grand time together. And why not? They're great kids, Andi."

She ducked her head. "I know. Sometimes, after they're asleep at night, I'm riddled with guilt because I spent the entire day nagging and preaching, instead of praising them for all the things they did right."

"There you go again. Beating yourself up for no reason." He caught her by the chin and lifted her face. Such a sweet face. So perfect, it had the breath catching in his throat. "They know you love them. They feel the same way about you."

"There are days when I'd give you a good argument about that."

"The three of you are simply caught in a storm right now. And all you can do is ride it out. Very soon you'll find yourselves in calm seas."

She couldn't hold back the sigh as she stepped back. "You make it sound so simple."

"Life's never simple. But there's no reason to complicate it further with guilt. You're doing the best you can. So are they."

She set her glass aside and touched her hands to her temples. "Please don't tell me I'll look back on this one day and laugh."

"What you've been through isn't funny. A hundred years from now it still won't be funny. But you will be able to look back one day and feel a sense of pride about how you handled it.''

"Promise?"

He nodded and set down his own glass. "Promise. Now, let me do that."

She looked up at him. "Do what?"

"Ease that headache."

"How did you...?"

Very gently he took hold of her hands and lowered them before pressing his thumbs to her temples, moving them in slow, rhythmic circles.

It was the most purely erotic feeling she'd ever known. With just the touch of his hands she could feel her entire body respond. Her heartbeat sped up. Her blood heated and her bones seemed to melt, until she marveled that her legs were still able to hold her.

Her voice was equally hypnotic. "When I was a kid my mother used to kiss away my hurts."

"I'll take that as an invitation."

"I didn't mean..."

"Shh."

She could feel the warmth of his breath on her cheek as he ever so softly brushed his mouth over her temple, her forehead, the tip of her nose. Without willing it, her eyes closed and she swayed toward him, offering her lips.

It seemed an eternity before he lowered his mouth to hers. When he did, there was an explosion of color behind her closed lids, and she felt as if the whole room dipped and swayed. She was forced to hold on to him for fear of falling.

He took the kiss deeper and heard her sigh as she gave herself up to it. The need for her was so sharp, so swift, if left him stunned and reeling.

"Donovan..." She started to push away.

"Wait." He wrapped his arms around her, drawing her closer, feeling her in every part of his body. "I'm not ready to let you go just yet. One more kiss."

"The children..."

He cut off her protest with a hard, quick kiss that had them both moaning with impatience as they strained to get closer.

Andi was shocked at her response. She had her hands on him, and she wanted, more than anything in the world, to crawl inside his skin, though she feared even that wouldn't be enough. The wanting was unlike anything she'd ever known. As compelling as the pull of the tide. Even though a part of her mind was sending warning signals, her body chose to ignore them. With each touch he took her higher. With each kiss, she was in deeper.

"Let's tell Mom."

At the sound of Cory's voice, Andi pulled away. She could hear the hurried footsteps as the children sprinted up on the porch. By the time the door slammed, she and Donovan had managed to step apart. But just barely. Their chests rose and fell with each ragged breath.

"Me first, Cory."

"Okay. Tell her."

"The carrots are all gone," Taylor said proudly.

"Oh, honey." Andi had to swallow twice to find her voice. "That's wonderful. I'll bet it was the woodchuck."

"Uh-huh. Isn't that great, Donovan?"

He fumbled for his wine, noting that his hand was unsteady. "It sure is. I told you he's shy. He likes to do his eating alone."

"Can I leave him more carrots tomorrow, Mama?"

"I don't see why not." Andi knew her cheeks were flushed, which only made her all the more uncomfortable.

She could see her son staring at her, and wondered if he could tell just by looking at her that she'd been kissing Donovan.

Kissing? As she reached for her wine she nearly laughed aloud. They hadn't been so much kissing as attacking each other. Devouring. It occurred to Andi that if her children hadn't been here, she and Donovan would already be rolling across the floor.

The image had her sweating.

Donovan noted her eyes were a little too bright and her cheeks were suffused with color.

He gave her a wink that had the color deepening. "I think I'll check my pasta sauce."

Cory started after him. "Can I help?"

"Sure. In fact, you can all help."

Delighted, Taylor danced ahead of her mother. At the door Donovan paused until Andi caught up with him.

As she brushed past he leaned close to whisper, "Don't forget where we left off."

She shot him a look. "If you're thinking of trying for a second inning, think again."

"An apt description, since we've gone way past first base." He grinned. "Our chaperones can't stay awake all night."

"I've got news for you. I'll be leaving with them right after dinner."

"Spoilsport."

It was her turn to grin. "Thanks to those…chaperones, I've come to my senses."

"Or lost them. Think of all the fun you'll be missing if you call off the game now." He brushed a curl behind her ear and felt her trembling response to his touch. "Speaking of innings, like the great Yogi Berra said, It ain't over til it's over."

Cory looked up from the kitchen table. "What are you two whispering about?"

"Baseball," Donovan said with a grin. "Now who likes Parmesan cheese on their pasta?"

"You make the best spaghetti in the world." Cory used a slice of garlic bread to wipe the last of the sauce from his plate.

"Thanks, Cory. But I'm afraid that honor goes to Pop."

"That's his grandfather," Cory explained to his mother. "Pop went to live with Donovan's family after his dad died."

"Yeah." Taylor nodded. "And he's still living there."

"Really?" Andi glanced from her son to her daughter. "And how would the two of you know so much about Donovan's life?"

Cory beamed with pride. "He told us while we helped him today. His grandfather was a policeman like his father. And Donovan became a policeman, too. Only he policed the whole planet."

Taylor turned to her brother. "Is that bigger than the world?"

The boy shrugged. "It means the same thing."

"Oh." Taylor noisily sipped the last of her soda through a straw. "Did you wear a uniform, Donovan?"

"My uniform was whatever the natives were wearing."

"What are natives?" Taylor pushed aside her empty glass.

"People who live in a particular place. Right now we're the natives of these hills."

"We are?" The little girl looked pleased.

"That's right. And I think it's time to give the natives their just dessert." He glanced around the table. "I have apples, strawberries or bananas. Unless a magic genie baked a cake while we were having our pasta."

"I'll have strawberries." Cory eyed the huge bowl of washed and stemmed berries on the kitchen counter.

"Me, too." Taylor watched as Donovan spooned them into bowls and added powdered sugar on top.

After filling two cups with coffee he led the way to the front porch, where they lingered, watching a spectacular sunset.

Afterward, they carried their dishes to the kitchen, where Andi insisted on helping with the cleanup.

"You made the dinner. The least I can do is load the dishwasher."

Cory deposited his bowl in the sink. "Donovan, do you mind if Taylor and I go in the other room and look at all your stuff?"

"Not at all. Help yourself." Donovan picked up a towel and waited only long enough to see the children through the doorway before joining Andi at the sink.

"I think there are enough things in the other room to hold their interest for a half hour or more." He gave her a killer smile that had her heart tumbling. "Care to take up where we left off before dinner?"

"Not on your life." She put a hand to his chest when he leaned close.

His smile grew. "Don't you want to put a little fun in your life?"

"Fun? Danger is not my idea of fun, Donovan. And I know now that I'll be taking my life in my hands whenever I kiss you."

"All the better. Tell the truth." He placed his hands on either side of her, pinning her against the counter. "Would you be satisfied with bland?"

She could feel the imprint of his body on hers. It had her breath backing up and her heart beating overtime. "I think bland would be preferable to heart attack."

He shocked her by placing his fingertips to the pulse that fluttered at her throat. At once her heart seemed to take one hard bounce before beating even faster. "Is that what you're afraid of? Your heart?"

"Yes." She pushed his hand aside and took several steps away, fighting for air. "In more ways than one. I'm not...ready for this, Donovan. In the past year I haven't even kissed a man, let alone..." She could feel the heat stain her face and lowered her head. "You know."

"Yeah." That only made her all the more desirable. What he wanted, more than anything, was to take her in his arms and tell her everything would be all right. What he did was merely touch a hand to her hair. "Let's see what the kids are up to."

They walked to the front room, where Taylor was playing with several colorful baskets.

Cory turned from Donovan's desk and held up the thick manila folder. His eyes were stormy; his voice, accusing. "What are you doing with all this stuff about my dad?"

Donovan glanced at Taylor, happily playing, and took care with his words. "I agreed to look into the case."

"Why? Are you a lawyer?"

"No. But I have some connections to people who can tell me things they might not be willing to tell your mother or your uncle."

Cory glanced beyond Donovan to his mother. "Did you know about this?"

She nodded. "Your uncle Champ told me, after he approached Donovan about doing this." She took a step toward him. "I hope you're not disappointed in me, Cory."

The boy turned and took his time replacing the file. When he turned back, some of the anger had drained away. "I don't mind, Mom. But I want to talk to Donovan. Alone."

She looked concerned. Still, she didn't know how to refuse his request. "All right." She turned to her daughter. "Taylor, put Donovan's things back now, honey. It's time to go."

"Okay." The little girl replaced the baskets, then took her mother's hand.

When they glanced at Donovan, he said, "Cory and I will be out in a minute."

Mother and daughter walked out onto the porch.

When they were alone, Cory said, "I'm glad you're going to prove that my dad wasn't a thief."

"That isn't what I agreed to do, Cory."

The boy looked puzzled. "I don't understand."

"I agreed to do some digging. But there are no guarantees. You need to understand that I could very well find out things about your dad that you and your mother would rather not know."

He saw the quick flash of fear. But then, in the blink of an eye, Cory lifted his chin. "I know what everybody thinks about my dad. But I know he was innocent."

Donovan found himself fervently hoping, for the boy's sake, that it was true. And maybe for his own sake, as well, he realized. Because the truth was, he was falling a little in love with the entire Brady family. The last thing he wanted was to become the bearer of bad tidings.

He dropped an arm around Cory's shoulders as he opened the door. "Come on. I'll drive all of you home."

Overhearing him, Andi paused on the top step of the porch, with Taylor in her arms. "Don't be silly. Then you'll have to walk all the way back here in the dark."

"I don't mind." He took Taylor from her and carried her to the van. "It's a perfect night for a walk. Besides," he added with a wink, "it'll take my mind off what I'd rather be doing."

Andi knew she was blushing and felt a wave of gratitude for the darkness.

But as Donovan drove them down the hill, she watched his hands, so sure and steady on the wheel. The thought of those hands holding her sent a fresh series of tremors along her spine.

She was grateful for the children. Without them along, she wasn't quite sure just how strong she would be against the temptation to take this game into extra innings.

But it wasn't a game, she reminded herself. With a man like Donovan Lassiter it was deadly serious.

Chapter 8

"Hi, Donovan." As he stepped out the back door with a sack of birdseed, Cory came walking around the side of his house, with Taylor trailing behind.

Just seeing them chased away the gloom that often came creeping over him in the night. It had been a curse he'd carried since childhood. "'Morning. What's up?"

"We came to see if you needed help with anything."

Now that they'd discovered just how many grand adventures he could describe, the two children had begun spending more time at his house than they did at their own. If only, he thought, their mother would do the same. But since the night of their kiss, she'd been scrupulously avoiding him.

Not that he could blame her. This past year had been a turbulent one for Andi Brady, and she needed time to sort through her emotions. But with every passing day, seeing her in her yard in a pair of sexy shorts or waving as he walked to the mailbox, he could feel the tug of desire growing. Seeing her wasn't enough. He wanted to touch her. To devour her. To fill himself with her until he was sated.

He pulled himself back from his thoughts and looked up with a smile. "Thanks. I guess I could use some help." He held out the sack so they could dig their hands in. "Just toss some out there. The birds will find it."

"I brought some carrots for my woodchuck, too." Taylor dug into her pocket and came up with a handful.

"You're going to spoil him. Pretty soon he'll forget how to hunt for his own food."

"That's what Mama said. She said wild things shouldn't be treated the same as tame ones."

Especially wild men, he thought with a frown. No wonder she was keeping her distance. He'd scared her. Hadn't she said as much? And why not? He was well aware of the fact that he was barely civilized.

"Think we could go for another hike in the woods?" Cory tossed a handful of seed.

"I guess so. If your mom says it's all right with her."

The boy brightened. "How about this afternoon?"

"Works for me." Donovan closed the bag and stored it in a cabinet. "How about Taylor?"

"She's too small. Besides, Mom's taking her to the dentist."

The little girl shivered before shrinking behind her brother's back.

To help her overcome her fears, Donovan arched a brow. "Would your dentist happen to be Doc Carrington?"

Taylor looked at Cory for confirmation. The boy nodded.

Donovan winked at Taylor. "I heard he gives out really neat toys."

"He does?" The little girl's smile returned. "I'd rather get a new toy than go walking through some old icky forest."

"Not me." Cory grabbed his sister's hand. "Come on. We've got to run." He called over his shoulder, "If Mom says yes, I'll be back."

"Okay. I'll be here." Donovan watched them go, before going off to hunt up his hiking boots.

He glanced fleetingly at his computer, then decided he hadn't wanted to work today, anyway. There'd be time enough for his book another day. Besides, he was actually looking forward to hiking. He enjoyed the solitude of the forest. It was one of the things that had lured him to this location in the first place.

An hour later he and Cory were deep in the woods and heading toward the waterfall.

"My dad and I used to go hiking on weekends." Cory scrambled down a narrow slope.

"Where?"

"We started with a park not far from our house. Then we hiked across some of the battlefields. My dad knew everything. The names of the battles and the generals. He was going to take me running with him when I got bigger." He glanced at Donovan. "Did you know that my dad ran track in college and almost made the Olympic team?"

"Yeah. I read that in his file. That's pretty impressive, isn't it?" It occurred to Donovan that Cory seemed relieved to know that he could speak freely to someone about his father. Now that he knew Donovan was working on his father's case, he felt free to confide his feelings. "You think you'll run track, too?"

Cory shrugged. "My dad thought soccer was my

sport. But I don't know. I'm a pretty good runner.
You think I could take after him?''

"You might. But it's tough trying to live up to
someone else's successes. Why not figure out what
you're dying to do and then do it?"

"That's what my dad said. He told me I should
always follow my dream. That's what he finally did.
He said he spent years trying to live up to my grandfather's plans for him. That's why my dad followed
him into the banking business. But my dad always
wanted to try something on his own and make it a
success."

Donovan felt a prickle of unease. Would Adam
Brady have gone so far as to steal in order to prove
to his father that he'd been right to leave the family
business? Would he do whatever it took to make a
success of his gamble, to justify himself to his family?

In his research of the criminal mind he'd learned
that greed wasn't the only factor driving men to
commit crime. Guilt could also be a strong motive.

"Wow."

His thoughts were interrupted by Cory's shout as
they caught their first glimpse of the waterfall.

The boy pointed. "Look at that, Donovan. A rainbow."

Sunlight filtered through the leaves of towering

trees to glisten on the spray of water, creating a colorful rainbow.

Donovan took his camera from around his neck and handed it to Cory. "Why don't you get a shot of that?"

"You mean it?"

Donovan nodded. "Take your time and frame the shot."

"What does that mean? 'Frame the shot'?"

"Look through the lens and keep moving back and forth until you see exactly what you want to see in your picture. Then hold it level and get a feel for how the scene will look when it's printed out."

The boy took a moment to adjust the viewfinder before snapping off a series of pictures. After handing back the camera, he climbed up on the big rock for a better view.

Donovan climbed up beside him, and the two of them stretched out, enjoying the call of birds, the rush of water, the peacefulness of the setting.

"On a day like this," Donovan remarked, "you'd almost think you were on a deserted island, with nobody around for miles."

Cory looked over at the man who lay faceup, eyes closed behind his sunglasses. "Were you ever on a deserted island?"

"Once or twice."

"What did you do there?"

"Mostly I took soil samples."

"What for?"

"To see if there had been any weapons tested recently."

"You mean like guns and missiles?"

Donovan sat up and watched a pair of ducks swimming in lazy circles around the pond. "There are other weapons. Other ways to destroy an opponent. Some leaders don't care how many innocent people are hurt, as long as they stay in power. They'll even develop and test chemicals or germs as weapons, without regard to their effect on fish, birds, animals and eventually people."

Although Cory was too young to understand the enormity of such weapons, he could tell, by the change in Donovan's tone, that this man cared deeply about such things.

"Are those leaders bad people?"

"Very bad."

"Did you stop them?"

Donovan looked over at the boy. "I'd like to think I did. But in my line of work I was rarely around long enough to learn the answer."

"Where did you go?"

"Off to another island or mountaintop or forest or country. Wherever I was needed."

"You never got to stay and fight the bad men?"

"That's for soldiers. And sometimes for ordinary people who decide they can't take any more. But I always thought I was doing my share by finding proof of the crimes in the first place." He lowered his voice. "Look."

The boy turned to see a doe and fawn step up to the water's edge. Out of the corner of his eye he saw Donovan slip the camera from around his neck and squeeze off several quick shots in succession.

They remained silent until the deer retreated, blending once more into the forest.

Cory turned to Donovan. "How'd you learn to snap pictures so fast, without even looking through the lens?"

"I guess it comes from practice. Sometimes, when I sensed danger, I often had to squeeze off shots with no time to frame them. I learned to trust my instincts." He handed the camera over to Cory. "Why don't you keep this for a while and practice."

"You don't mind?"

"Go ahead."

The boy was so delighted he jumped up and began snapping shots of everything that caught his interest. An odd-shaped boulder. A tree growing out of the trunk of a fallen log. A family of geese that circled the pond before coming in for a noisy landing.

They followed a new trail back, and Donovan showed Cory how to read a compass and how to mark his trail.

"If you don't want anyone else to follow your trail, you have to use something that looks natural to anyone except you."

"How?" the boy asked.

Donovan pointed to some stones. "It could be as simple as setting one stone on top of another, or lining them up like arrows to point the way." He reached up to some low-handing branches of a tree. "You could use a pocket knife to make a notch in the trunk of a tree, or, if you thought you were being followed, you could simply bend the twigs in a pattern that nobody else would notice." As he was speaking he twisted a supple young twig into a simple figure eight.

"Wow." Cory was impressed. "Have you ever been lost?"

"Yeah." Donovan thought back over the years. After losing his father, he'd been a lost child and had spent years trying to find himself. Even the name he'd given the group of soldiers of fortune who had been his friends had reflected that loss. "But I've always believed I could find my way

back. And you can, too, Cory. You just have to believe in yourself.''

As they stepped out of the woods and started
along the gravel path toward their homes, Cory
lifted the strap from around his neck. "Here's your
camera. Thanks for letting me use it."

Donovan shook his head. "Keep it."

The boy stopped in his tracks, his mouth open in
surprise. "You mean it?"

"Yeah." Donovan couldn't help chuckling at the
look of pure astonishment on the boy's face. "I saw
those pictures you snapped last time we were in the
woods. They're good. I think you might have a future in photography."

As Cory moved along beside Donovan, he wasn't
certain if his feet were touching the ground. When
they reached his house he went dashing inside,
shouting, "Mom. I'm home."

Andi walked into the kitchen. When she realized
her son wasn't alone, she felt her cheeks grow hot.
"Hi, Donovan."

"Andi." He remained by the door.

"Look what Donovan gave me." Cory held out
the camera.

Andi took the camera from his hand and looked
it over, then shot a look at the man before shaking
her head. "This is far too expensive..."

"Too late." Donovan held up a hand to cut off her protest. "I've already given it to him."

"But this is…"

"A gift. From me to Cory. There's nothing you can say that will change my mind." He grinned at the little girl who came dashing down the stairs. "How was your visit with Doc Carrington?"

"I sat really still in the chair while he counted my teeth. And he said I was so good I could choose two toys from the toy chest."

"Two? I'm impressed. So, what did you pick?"

She reached into the pocket of her pink-checked jeans and pulled out a little duck. "You wind him up and he walks across the table and says quack." While she was explaining, she proudly gave a demonstration.

"Pretty neat." Donovan was grinning from ear to ear. "What else did you get?"

"This." She dug in her other pocket and retrieved a tiny lipstick.

He arched a brow. "Is that real lipstick or just pretend?"

"It's real gloss," the girl said proudly. "It tastes like bubble gum."

"So do you wear it or eat it?"

Taylor giggled. "I wear it. But Mama says I can only wear it on special occasions."

"Like on your sixteenth birthday?"

"You're silly." Taylor dissolved in giggles.

At the sound of her daughter's laughter Andi realized just how much she'd missed this. And missed the man who brought such joy to her children.

She looked over at Donovan. "I hope you'll stay and eat with us. I brought pizza from town."

"Pizza." Cory stopped examining his camera long enough to declare, "I'm starving."

Donovan nodded. "Now that you mention it, so am I."

"You'll stay?" Andi's smile bloomed. "It'll just take a few minutes to heat it up."

"While you're doing that, the kids and I will set the table, right after we wash up." He turned to Cory. "Think you can tear yourself away from the camera long enough to lend a hand?"

Reluctantly Cory set the camera aside and went to wash. Afterward the two children helped Donovan set the table. By the time the pizza was hot, their mouths were watering.

While Donovan passed around the hot slices, Andi filled a platter with sizzling fries. Except for a few sighs of pleasure, the four of them fell silent as they devoured their meal.

After his third slice, Donovan leaned back and sipped strong hot coffee. "There were times when

I would be in a jungle eating nuts and berries, or in a peasant village eating rice and beans, and I'd find myself so hungry for pizza I could almost taste it.''

Taylor nibbled stringy cheese. ''Why didn't you just order some?''

''They don't have pizza shops in jungles, Taylor,'' Cory said importantly.

''They don't?'' Taylor looked to Donovan for confirmation.

''Cory's right. There are plenty of little towns and villages in the world where they've never even heard of fast food.''

''What do they eat when their mamas don't want to cook?''

Donovan chuckled. ''I hope you never have to find out.'' Just then his smile widened when Andi placed bowls of chocolate ice cream in front of them, along with a dish of chocolate chip cookies.

''Double chocolate.'' Donovan dipped a spoon in the ice cream, then bit into a cookie. ''It doesn't get much better than this.''

Across the table Andi found herself thinking the same thing. The sound of her children's laughter was like a soothing balm to her wounded soul. All it took was a word from this man and the children changed before her eyes. Today was a perfect example. All the way to town Taylor had speculated on the toys in Doc Carrington's office. Not once had she worried about meeting a stranger. And all because of the seed Donovan had planted.

After dinner the four of them worked together clearing the table and loading the dishwasher, before the children headed out on the back porch.

"There's coffee left, Donovan." Andi held up a clean cup. "Want some?"

"Sure." When she handed him the coffee their fingers brushed. Instead of pulling away, she paused to lay a hand over his. "Thanks for taking Cory hiking today. He was so excited. But the camera…"

He stopped her with a finger to her lips that had something dark and dangerous flaring in his eyes. "I want him to have it."

"All right." She stood perfectly still, wishing it were his mouth on hers, instead of his finger.

She wondered if he could read the desire in her eyes.

"Mama." At the sound of Taylor's shout, both she and Donovan hurried to the porch.

Taylor pointed to the darkness. "Mama, I saw a little light."

"I saw one, too." Cory was out of his chair and racing to the edge of the porch.

Seconds later they saw another one and then another.

"What are they?" Cory asked.

"Fireflies." Donovan leaned a hip against the porch railing. "When we were kids, my brothers and sister and I used to catch them in jars and watch them light up."

"You did?" Cory turned. "Could we try?"

"I don't see why not." Andi left, returning minutes later with two glass jars. "Just remember that you if you catch any, you have to turn them loose after they've performed their little trick for you."

"We will." Cory handed a jar to his little sister, and the two dashed out into the darkness, chasing the tiny lights.

Suddenly Cory shouted, "I caught one."

The two children hurried up on the porch, and the four of them gathered around, watching as the tiny firefly gave off its sparks, lighting up the jar.

"It really does light up." Cory was as fascinated as his little sister.

After a few minutes Andi said, "I think you'd better set this little firefly free."

Cory took his hand away from the top and the insect flew off, leaving little sparks of light in its wake.

"Will you help me catch one now, Cory?" Taylor held up her empty jar.

"Sure. Come on." Cory took her by the hand, and the two of them danced across the backyard.

Andi settled down on a glider, listening to the sound of her children's laughter.

When Donovan joined her he touched a finger to her cheek. "What's this? Tears?"

She sniffed. "Happy tears. Listen."

He lifted his head. "I don't hear anything except the kids."

"That's just it. For so long now all I heard was whining and complaining, and often, late at night, the sound of their crying. In just these few short weeks all our lives have changed. Taylor used to hide behind my skirts whenever she had to meet anyone new. Today she shook the dentist's hand and sat quietly in the chair while he examined her teeth. And Cory." She shook her head. "He's been so unhappy for so long. And suddenly it's as though the sun has come out after a year of angry storm clouds."

"I'm glad." He set aside his empty cup and drew an arm around her shoulders. "So. Now that you've described your children, what about their mother? How're you holding up, Andi?"

She turned to him with shining eyes. "Don't you see? If they're happy, I'm happy. I can't bear to see them suffering. And it's all because of you, Donovan. Ever since we came here and met you, our lives have changed.''

''I wish I could take the credit. But the truth is, since meeting the three of you, my life has changed for the better, too.''

''Really?''

''Yeah. Really.'' He tipped up her face and brushed his mouth over hers.

The rush of heat was so intense, he felt as though he'd been thrust into a furnace. The need for this woman was an ache, sharp and deep, that had him sucking in a breath on the pain.

Against her lips he whispered, ''You know I want you, Andi.''

''I know.'' She lifted a hand to his cheek and moved back so she could look into his eyes. ''What frightens me is that I want you, too.''

She saw the quirk of his lips before he pressed his forehead to hers. ''That's a relief. I'd hate to think this was a one-sided relationship.''

''It isn't a relationship.'' She drew back, hating the way her body strained toward his. Even now, with a single kiss, she had to struggle against the most amazing tug of desire that had her blood heating, her bones melting.

''What is it?'' He reached over, twirling a strand of her hair around his finger.

"It's a friendship, I hope. And maybe, in time, it can be more."

"Time." He couldn't hide the frustration in his voice.

"I need time, Donovan. Time to grieve my loss. Time to help my children through their own grief. And time to be sure that what I'm feeling isn't just loneliness." The mere touch of his hand on her hair had ribbons of fire and ice curling along her spine. Her voice trembled. "How would you feel if you found out that I'd used you to satisfy my own needs?"

His smile was quick and dangerous. "I'm willing to sacrifice my body, if that's what it takes."

"Oh, you." She framed his face with her hands. "What am I going to do with you?"

"You could start by kissing me."

She brushed her lips over his, intending a light, teasing kiss. But the moment their lips met, everything changed. One moment they were laughing. The next they were locked in an embrace that had all the breath backing up in their lungs as they took the kiss deeper.

Andi gave herself up to the pleasure. Oh, it felt so good to be held in these strong, capable arms. So right to be here with this man.

"Mama. Donovan." Little Taylor's voice had them moving apart. "I finally caught one. Look."

The little girl came rushing up the steps with Cory behind her. "Look at the light."

Donovan and Andi went through the motions of watching the firefly, until at last the children released it to the darkness. But all the while they felt the electric charge that shot between them each time they touched.

A short time later, as Donovan walked along the gravel path to his house, his thoughts were as dark as the night that closed around him. He'd never wanted anything, or anyone, as desperately as he wanted Andi Brady. But she was right, of course. If this relationship were to move to another level, the choice had to be hers.

He just hoped he didn't slowly go mad while she made up her mind.

Chapter 9

It was barely dawn, but Donovan had been up for hours feeling tense and edgy. He'd been reading through the Adam Brady file before going to bed. Something he'd read had begun playing through his mind while he slept. It was a pattern in his life since early childhood. At rest, his mind took over and worked through whatever knotty problems he had to deal with, until all the tangles were gradually unraveled. Now he found himself wide-awake and sifting through the report again.

He flipped through another page, then stopped and reread the paragraph a second time. His eyes narrowed in thought. It wasn't much. But it was a question that needed answering. He tapped a pencil against the desktop. This wasn't something he could accomplish by going through channels.

He booted up his computer and sent an e-mail to an old friend who still had access to government files. There was no way of knowing when, or even if he would get a reply.

Rubbing a hand over the stubble on his chin he headed toward the bathroom to shave and shower. Half an hour later, while he sipped fresh coffee, he checked his e-mails and found an answer.

His fingers flew over the keys as he responded. After several more e-mail exchanges, he shut down his computer. As he reached for the keys to his car he was shaking his head in amazement. It would seem his fellow patriots, who had once called themselves The Lost, were still connected. If only by the slimmest of threads.

"Mom." Cory slammed into the house and held out a wrinkled piece of paper. "Donovan isn't home. This was taped to his door."

Andi read the handwritten note:

"Gone to D.C. Don't know when I'll be back."

Cory was reading over her shoulder, though he already knew what it said. He looked crestfallen. "Why didn't he tell us?"

"Maybe something came up unexpectedly." She managed a smile, even though she was as distressed as her son. "After all, he doesn't owe us an explanation every time he makes a move."

"I know. But he didn't say a word about this last night."

She was thinking the same thing. Aloud she merely said, "I've been meaning to scrub the barbecue. I think this would be a good day to tackle it. Want to help?"

He shrugged. She could see that his heart wasn't in it. Neither was hers. But she'd always found solace in work. Maybe it would help Cory to stay busy.

"Come on," she coaxed. "Afterward, I'll cook burgers."

"Okay. I guess." Cory glanced at the note again, then walked away.

Suddenly all the joy had gone out of his day.

As Donovan turned off the highway and drove through the little town of Prattsville, he touched a hand to the dark growth that shadowed his lower face.

He hadn't expected to be gone for three days. But once he got to D.C. he knew he wasn't going to leave until he had all the information he wanted. It had been far from easy. If not for his old connections, it would have been impossible to access the government's files and come up with some of the material that was listed as classified.

Donovan had mastered the art of using his clout only when it was absolutely necessary. There were plenty of people in Washington who owed him favors. He rarely called in his markers. But when he did, old friends responded and seemed almost gleeful at the prospect of breaking a few rules. After all, that had been one of the traits that had brought them all together in the first place. Their ability to think on their feet, to defy logic, to question authority, had brought them to the attention of a top-secret organization hoping to recruit enthusiastic members. Donovan and his cohorts had seen themselves standing tall and proud against any and all aggressors. Even, at times, their own government bureaucracy.

He turned onto the gravel path and slowed his car when he saw two figures up ahead.

Cory and Taylor looked up, then started running toward him.

"Donovan. You're back." Taylor's voice was high-pitched with excitement. "Mama. Look. Donovan's back."

Andi was sweeping the front porch. She set aside her broom and walked out to the road, hoping she didn't look too eager to see him.

"Hi." Donovan brought his car to a stop and lowered the window.

Taylor stood on tiptoe to peer inside the car. "Where'd you go, Donovan?"

"I had some business in D.C."

"We missed you. Didn't we, Mama?"

Andi had no chance to reply before Taylor said, "We were afraid you were never coming back. Weren't we, Cory?"

"Yeah. You were gone a long time, Donovan." The boy's tone was accusing. He was studying the dark beard that covered the man's cheeks and chin, and the rumpled clothing that gave him the look of something untamed and more than a little dangerous. "Did you sleep in your car?"

"At a friend's place." Donovan was working hard at not staring at Andi. But it wasn't easy. She looked so good. She was wearing some kind of pink gauzy shirt that clung to her breasts and was tied at her midriff. Below that were shorts in the same material. Between the shorts and blouse was a tantalizing expanse of pale flesh.

"A girlfriend?" Taylor asked innocently.

Andi's hand paused midway to her throat.

"No. A guy I used to work with."

She felt her heart resume beating. And though she wasn't aware of it, her smile was back. "If you haven't had dinner yet, we were getting ready to eat. I'm making fried chicken.''

''And biscuits.'' Taylor added.

Donovan touched a hand to his beard. ''Do I have time to go up to the house and shave?''

Andi hoped she didn't look as eager as her children. ''Take all the time you want.''

''Can Cory and I go along?'' Taylor turned pleading eyes toward her mother.

She was shaking her head. ''I don't want you pestering—''

Donovan gave her a quick smile. ''Let them come. They can open up the house and let in some air while I clean up.''

She relented. ''As long as you don't mind.''

Cory was already opening the car door and helping his little sister inside to ensure that their mother didn't have a change of heart. With their seat belts fastened, they waved as Donovan pulled away.

Taylor turned to watch her mother climb the steps of the porch. ''Mama missed you, Donovan.''

''Now how would you know that?''

''She talked about you a lot. And sometimes when she thought we weren't looking, she'd stare up the hill at your house.''

Donovan had to take a moment for his heart to

settle. Thank heaven for little tattlers. "I missed her, too. I missed all of you."

"You did?"

He was aware of two pairs of honey eyes watching him in the rearview mirror with a hunger that did strange things to his heart. One of them looked hopeful. The other looked as angry and hurt as ever. "Yeah. I did. A lot."

Minutes later Cory and Taylor were climbing out of his car and racing ahead to the porch, where they waited until he retrieved his battered duffel from the trunk.

Once inside they ran around opening windows and doors, letting in the fresh air, while Donovan headed toward his bedroom.

Over his shoulder he called, "I'll be a new man in a few minutes."

He proved to be as good as his word. With his face clean-shaven and his dark hair still dripping from the shower, he was dressed in charcoal slacks and a matching polo shirt when he stepped from the room.

"Ah." He breathed deeply. "Now the house smells fresh again. Thanks to the two of you. Ready to go to dinner?"

The two children hurried ahead of him to the car. He followed along more slowly before climbing in behind the wheel. Minutes later he parked his car beside Andi's van and retrieved something from his trunk. As the children started toward the house they noticed a bulging shopping bag in his hands.

"What's in the bag?" Taylor asked.

"Surprises."

"For us?" Taylor's eyes were wide with excitement.

"Could be."

He followed them into the kitchen, where Andi was busy filling a platter with fried chicken. Once again he felt the jolt at the sight of those long, long legs, and that tempting bit of flesh exposed at her midriff. "Need some help?"

She paused to give him a smile, surprised at the change in him. Gone was the rumpled look of an hour ago. But though he was clean-shaven and dressed in the latest fashion, there was still something dangerous about him. Maybe it was the look in his eyes as he studied her. Like a wolf that had just picked up the scent of prey. It made her heart jittery.

"Thanks, Donovan. I can manage."

Taylor eyed the bag in his hand. "Donovan's got a surprise."

"For you, honey?"

The little girl was twitching with excitement. "I don't know. Is it for me, Donovan?"

With a wink he reached inside and brought out a wrapped package. "This one's for you, Taylor."

She tore off the wrapping and opened the cover of a big box, then removed layers of pink tissue to reveal a basket of stuffed animals. A spotted dog with soulful eyes and a white fluffy cat sporting a pink bow around its neck. To Taylor's delight, wedged between them was a brown woodchuck with a toothy grin.

"Oh, Donovan." The little girl threw herself into his arms and hugged him fiercely.

Caught off guard by her reaction, he wrapped his arms around her and held her close for long moments, wondering at the strange pounding of his heartbeat.

When at last he released her he gave her a big smile. "I figured they could be your pets. Just until you get those allergies under control."

"I love them. Look, Mama." Taylor picked up the basket and held it out for her mother's inspection.

"Oh, my. A dog, a cat and a woodchuck. That's quite a collection of pets."

"They're going to sleep with me tonight. And

every night," she said, hugging each stuffed animal in turn.

Donovan reached into the bag and pulled out a second, smaller box. "This one's for you, Cory."

The boy seemed stunned that he was getting something. For the longest time he merely stared at the box, then up at Donovan's face. Finally he lifted the lid and stared at a scarred and battered round metal disk encased in tissue. "What's this?"

"A compass." Donovan watched as the boy turned it over.

Cory looked up. "What do the letters *R. L.* stand for?"

"Riordan Lassiter. It belonged to my father."

"You're giving me your father's compass?"

Donovan nodded. "You're getting pretty good at navigating the woods. With that along as your guide, you'll always find your way back home. I ought to know. I've carried it with me through dozens of countries. Through jungles and mountains and deserts."

The importance of this gift suddenly dawned on Cory. But all he said was, "That's pretty neat." He thought briefly about throwing himself into Donovan's arms the way his little sister had, but he managed to hold back. Instead he stuck out his hand. "Thanks, Donovan."

Donovan solemnly shook the boy's hand. "You're welcome."

Cory fastened it to the belt loop of his shorts. "I guess I'll carry it with me all the time, just like you."

Taylor glanced at the shopping bag. "Did you bring something for Mama, too?"

"Now, Taylor." Andi looked embarrassed.

"As a matter of fact, I think there is something in here for her." Donovan reached to the bottom of the bag and retrieved a small ivory box, which he handed to Andi.

"I can't imagine what this could be." She was blushing furiously as the two children gathered around to watch her open it. Inside the ivory case was a small, sky-blue music box with clouds floating across the top. When she lifted the lid it began to play a hauntingly beautiful song.

Andi was so startled she was forced to blink back tears. For a moment she was afraid to speak. Afraid if she did, she would embarrass herself. When she was certain she had her emotions under control she looked up at him with shiny eyes. "Oh, Donovan. This is…" She shook her head, unable to continue.

Taylor touched a hand to hers. "Don't you like it, Mama?"

"I love it, honey."

"Are you crying?"

"Of course not."

"What's that song?"

Still not trusting her voice, Andi looked to Donovan for help.

"It's something from a long time ago. Something your grandparents would probably recognize. It's called 'Beautiful Dreamer.'"

Andi sniffed and set the music box on the counter before taking a deep breath. "I think this calls for a celebration. I have some champagne in here somewhere."

She began rummaging around in a cupboard, until Donovan crossed to her side and reached a hand over her head to lift down a slim bottle. "Is this what you were looking for?"

Hearing his voice so close beside her, she went very still and turned. Their bodies brushed. Just the merest touch, but she was absolutely shattered by the feelings that ripped through her.

"Yes. I'll…open it." She didn't move. Couldn't.

"I'll do it." He continued standing there, the champagne forgotten as he stared down into her eyes.

The need for her was so sharp, so deep, it took all of his willpower not to kiss her. Knowing the children were watching, he allowed himself nothing more than the touch of a hand to her cheek. She moved against it like a kitten and murmured a sigh that had all the air backing up in his lungs.

"Donovan." She closed her eyes a moment and pressed a hand to his chest to steady herself.

"Shh." He lifted her hand to his lips, sending her heart into a series of dizzying somersaults.

"Are we ready to eat, Mom?"

At the sound of Cory's voice they both turned with matching looks of surprise mingled with guilt.

"I'll...be right there."

While she filled two glasses with milk, Donovan popped the cork on the champagne.

Minutes later they were gathered around the table. While Taylor regaled Donovan with tales of what she and her brother had done for the past three days, he sipped his champagne and struggled to pay attention. All during the meal he kept glancing at the woman seated across from him.

In his whole life he'd never wanted anything or anyone the way he wanted her. That was hard for a man like Donovan Lassiter to swallow. But as much as he wanted her, he knew the choice had to be hers alone. Hadn't he vowed to give her all the time she needed?

Still, with each passing minute, he began to think the waiting might be the death of him.

Chapter 10

"More chicken, Donovan?" Andi held the platter toward him.

"No, thanks." He glanced down at his plate and was amazed to see it empty. He couldn't remember eating a bite. Nor could he recall a single thing they'd talked about.

"Would you like coffee?" Without waiting for a reply, she was up and heading across the kitchen.

"I'll get it." He walked beside her and reached for the coffeepot at the same moment she did.

Their hands met, then froze.

Donovan stared down into her eyes and felt himself drowning in those honey depths. "I should go."

"No." She said it quickly. "I mean…the children have been missing you so much."

"I've missed them, too." His tone softened. "I missed their mother even more."

"Well." She picked up the coffeepot, praying she wouldn't spill any as she filled his cup. "I made chocolate parfait for dessert."

Donovan shook his head. "I never thought I'd see the day when I'd refuse chocolate, but I couldn't eat a bite."

Andi touched a hand to her stomach to calm her nerves. "I feel the same way." She handed each of her children a dessert and said, "Maybe you'd like to eat it on the back porch."

Donovan thought about keeping her here all to himself and giving in to the need to hold her. Instead he took a deep breath and followed Cory and Taylor out the door, where he settled on the top step, leaning his back against the rail while he sipped his coffee. Cory sat below him on the next step, while Taylor chose the glider alongside her mother.

Andi nudged off her shoes and wiggled her toes before giving a contented sigh.

The sun had already set behind the hills, leaving the sky streaked with ribbons of purple and pink and mauve. There was a sweet, clean taste to the breeze that whispered through the leaves of the trees. It was a perfect summer evening.

Donovan studied a freshly painted arbor across the yard, abloom with pale-pink roses. "I don't remember that being here before."

Andi smiled. "It was old and faded, so I gave it a fresh coat of paint. Then I just tied up the roses here and there where they'd fallen to the ground, and I'm amazed at how different it looks."

"You seem to have a magic touch." He nodded toward the flower gardens, abloom with foxglove and delphinium and sweet peas in a riot of texture and color. "That looks like it took some doing."

"I love flowers. And I've never minded hard work. In fact, the greater the challenge, the harder I dig in."

He fell silent, mulling her words. It occurred to him that they were quite a pair. All his life he'd embraced challenge. There was just something perverse in his nature that had him always eager to push the envelope. But he'd never before given much thought to the challenge of mundane household chores. He was beginning to see them in a whole new light.

Taylor polished off the last bite of parfait and looked over at her mother. "Can I take my new pets upstairs now and get them ready for bed?"

"So soon?"

"I never had pets to sleep with before. Please, Mama."

"Of course, honey."

"When we're ready to be tucked in, can Donovan come upstairs and see them?"

Andi merely nodded, too surprised to say a word.

Cory set aside his empty dish and held up his compass. "I can't wait to try this in the forest. Think we could go hiking tomorrow, Donovan?"

"I think I could spare a couple of hours." Donovan drained his cup and set it aside, leaning back to look up at the stars. He pointed. "There's the world's first compass."

The boy looked confused. "What do you mean? The sky?"

"The stars. Ancient sailors were able to navigate the whole world with only the stars to guide them."

"Do you think sailors could still do that today?"

"You bet. The stars, like that compass, are constant."

"What does that mean?"

"It means they never change. They're in a fixed place in the heaven. And no matter where you are, you can find your way back by following your star."

Cory stifled a yawn. "Will you tell me the names of the stars?"

"I will." Donovan grinned. "Another night. I think you'd better get to bed before you fall asleep right here on the porch."

"Yeah." Cory got up and started up the steps. As he passed Donovan he paused. "I'm…glad you're back."

"So am I."

Just then they heard Taylor calling from her room. "Mama. Donovan. Come up and say good-night."

They followed Cory into the house and up the stairs.

Andi led the way to Taylor's room.

Inside, the little girl was already snuggled into her bed, with the spotted dog and white cat on one side of her pillow and the woodchuck on the other.

"I've given them names," Taylor announced solemnly. "My dog is Spot, my kitty is Snowflake, and my woodchuck is Woody."

"Very inventive." Donovan swallowed back his smile.

She held them up. "If you'd like, you can both kiss them good-night."

Andi and Donovan took turns kissing the animals.

"Now me." Taylor puckered her lips and kissed them both, then wrapped her arms around Donovan's neck and hugged him fiercely. "I love my new pets, Donovan."

"I'm glad, Taylor. I can see that they love being here with you. I just hope they don't keep you up tonight while they get used to their new home."

She giggled at his little joke.

After switching off her light, Andi moved to her son's room.

"Ready for bed?" she called.

"Just about." Cory was dressed in his pajamas and kneeling at the window, staring up at the darkened sky. He turned and caught sight of his mother and Donovan in the doorway. The sight of them together gave him a funny feeling. It wasn't, he realized, a bad feeling. But seeing them together made him feel safe. "I was thinking how glad I am that I have this." He opened his hand to reveal his new compass. "So I won't ever have to rely on the stars to help me find my way back home." He climbed into bed, and Andi hurried across the room to kiss him good-night.

He looked over at the man in the doorway. In the shadows he couldn't see his face clearly. Maybe, if he squeezed his eyes really tight, Donovan would turn into his father. "'Night, Donovan."

"Good night, Cory."

He watched as his mother switched off his light and joined Donovan in the hall before pulling the door shut. For the last three nights the little boy's sleep had been tormented by frightening dreams. But now that Donovan was back, he could feel the fears beginning to slip away.

He was asleep before they descended the stairs.

Donovan was strangely silent as he followed Andi to the kitchen.

She padded barefoot across the room before turning to him with a smile. ''More coffee?''

''No, thanks.'' His tone was gruff as he started toward the door. ''It's time for me to leave.''

''I wish you wouldn't.''

''Look, Andi, I…''

''Stay a while longer, Donovan.'' She laid a hand over his. It was the simplest gesture, but she saw something dark and dangerous in his eyes as he drew back.

''It wouldn't be safe to stay. Not with the kids asleep upstairs, and the two of us alone down here.''

''No, it wouldn't be safe.'' She twisted her hands together, fighting nerves. ''I've always played it safe. All my life I've followed the rules. I floss every night.''

Despite the tension building inside him, his voice warmed with unspoken laughter. ''It shows in your smile.''

There was no answering smile from Andi. In fact, she looked achingly sad. ''You don't understand. I buckle my seat belt. I don't cross streets against the light. I eat my vegetables, knowing they're good for me. I'm a conscientious mother.''

He nodded, not sure where this was leading. "The best."

She gave a long sad sigh that seemed to come from deep within. "And I find myself wanting a man who, if rumors are to be believed, has never once played by the rules."

His eyes narrowed. He was like a coiled snake as he caught her roughly by the upper arms and held her a little away. "Say that again."

She shrugged aside her fear and stiffened her spine. "I said, if rumors are to be believed—"

"Not that." His voice was hard as nails. "The first part."

Her eyes went wide at the change she could sense in him. It took her a moment to recall just what she'd said. When she did, the fear drained away, replaced by the sudden realization that he wasn't so much angry as disbelieving. "I said I find myself wanting—" she had to stop and swallow hard "—wanting you."

He pinned her with a look that had her heart stuttering. "You're sure?"

"Yes." She nodded for emphasis. "This isn't

easy for me to admit. But I...want you, Donovan. Desperately.''

"Desperately.'' He closed his eyes, needing a moment to absorb the blow to his heart. "Desperately.'' He said it a second time, almost like a prayer. "So, I'm not alone in this.'' When he opened his eyes, they fixed on hers like a laser. "Do you understand where this is leading?''

Her chin came up. "I'm not an innocent, Donovan. After all, I've been married. I know about the things men and women do.''

His teeth flashed in a heart-stopping grin. "You only think you do. You don't have any idea about where I want to take you.''

"I'm a big girl now.'' Her heart was slamming against her ribs, making her feel like anything but an adult. "I know what I want. I want you, Donovan.''

"How can you? You don't even know me.''

"Then...I'll get to know you. And you'll get to know me.''

There was a long moment of silence before he spoke. "I've waited so long for this, I can't promise to be gentle, Andi.''

She lifted her hands to either side of his face. "I don't need you to be gentle. I just need you, Donovan.''

He muttered an oath. The touch of her hands was his undoing. He remained as still as a statue, struggling to bank the fire that was racing through his veins and straight to his loins. Then he gave up the battle within himself.

In one smooth motion he scooped her up and whispered against her temple, "And I need you. Now. This minute." He kicked open the door and carried her outside and down the porch.

"Donovan." She looked around in alarm. "Where are you taking me?"

His smile was quick and dangerous. "To the rose arbor. If we're noisy, it's far enough away from the house that we won't wake the kids."

"Noisy?"

He turned his head, capturing her mouth with his, and heard her whimper. The sound of it sent his heart into overdrive.

"I don't know about you, but I'm so revved I'm apt to howl at the moon."

That had her chuckling, until he set her on her feet and covered her mouth in a kiss so hot, so hungry, it stole the very breath from her lungs. Her laughter was gone, replaced by a long, deep sigh.

His arms came around her, holding her to the length of him, alerting her to the fact that he was fully aroused.

"I've been like a crazy man, Andi. Watching you all evening. Wanting you. Wanting to touch you. Like this." He ran his fingers up her sides until they encountered the bare flesh at her midriff. He felt her quivering response the moment he made contact.

"It was the same for me." She dug her fingers into his hair and poured herself into the kiss. "I couldn't wait to get my hands on you."

He moved his hands upward to the soft swell of her breasts, where his thumbs teased and stroked. "I'd pretty much convinced myself that I'd be doing you a favor to keep my distance."

With each stroke of his thumbs she felt her breath catch in her throat. Her words tumbled out between pursed lips. "I felt the same way, until I realized these past three days just how empty my life had become with you away."

"My entire life has been empty—" the look he sent her was smoldering "—until this moment." He feasted on her lips, filling himself with the taste of her. He heard her little moan of pleasure as he ran hot, wet kisses down the smooth column of her throat.

She smelled soap-and-water clean. As fresh as springtime. And as sexy as sin. He wanted to devour her in a single bite. Instead, he forced himself to go slowly, to savor every moment.

He kept his eyes steady on hers as he unbuttoned her blouse and fiddled with the tie at her midriff. He slid it from her shoulders to reveal a bit of lace that barely covered her breasts. Skimming a finger between the darkened cleft he parted the bra before tossing it aside.

"I've waited so long to see you like this." He brushed soft butterfly kisses across her shoulder, then lower, to the swell of her breast. "So long."

The feel of his lips against her skin had the blood roaring in her temples. She thought her legs would surely fail her. She brought her arms around his waist and clung to him as her bones began to melt like hot wax. Her whole body was trembling, vibrating with need.

"Hold on to me, Andi." He whispered the words against her throat as he began to take her in like a man starved for the taste of her.

She did as he asked, helpless to do more than cling while his mouth, that warm, clever mouth, drove her slowly mad. Her heart was thundering. A wild, primitive beat that pulsed through her veins and fluttered at her throat like a caged bird.

At last he lifted his head, giving her a moment to settle.

Frantic to touch him as he was touching her, she tore at his shirt, tugging it over his head. When she reached for the snaps at his waist, he helped her, kicking aside the rest of his clothes with a hiss of frustration.

He had the most amazing body. Her throat went dry at the sight of all those hard, corded muscles.

"I love it when you touch me, Andi. Touch me again." His words were a fierce whisper.

She did as he asked, pleasuring them both by running her hands over him with a boldness she never would have believed possible.

"I need to see you. All of you." He reached a hand to the waist of her gauzy shorts and tugged them free in one smooth motion. Her lacy briefs weren't treated with the same care as he tore them aside in his haste, before dragging her roughly against him, flesh to flesh.

His kisses weren't tender. His touches weren't gentle. He was fully, completely engaged, and would allow no less of her. It occurred to Andi that he made love the same way he'd always lived his life. On the wild side. Dark and dangerous. Raw and primitive. And so exciting she could feel herself almost exploding with the most amazing feelings.

The air around them seemed to become hot and thick, until every breath was labored. He drew her down to the cool grass, but it offered no comfort from the heat that seared her flesh and clogged her lungs. She watched him through a mist of passion as he moved over her, taking her higher than she'd ever been. He reminded her of a fierce jungle creature, all muscle and sinew, his beautiful body glistening in the moonlight.

Her sighs bordered on sobs as he nibbled his way down her body, taking her on a wild, dizzying ride before bringing her to the first shocking crest.

He heard her gasp at the same moment that he felt her body shudder. Stunned, she clutched him and sobbed out his name.

"Donovan. Donovan." She whispered his name like a prayer.

"Oh, Andi. I've dreamed of seeing you like this. Dreamed of this. Only this."

She'd thought he would take her now, and end this madness that held them both in its grip. But he wanted more. So much more. And so he gave her no time to recover before taking her even higher, until they were both feeling dazed and more than a little breathless.

From somewhere nearby a night bird called, and from the woods its mate answered. A high, clear note hung in the air before fading. The man and woman locked in each other's arms were oblivious. A soft summer breeze rippled the leaves of the trees and brought with it the fragrance of roses. In the brush nearby an animal scurried for cover as Andi and Donovan lay in the grass, their bodies slick with sweat, their breathing labored.

The world had narrowed to this place and this moment, as they lost themselves in the wonder of each other and the all-consuming desire that drove them. Even the moon and stars seemed to have dimmed, to give them the privacy they craved.

Each time he thought he would surely have to take her, he found a newer, sharper hunger that demanded to be fed. And so he gave and took and gave, feeling the crest of desire grow and grow until it threatened to explode.

Blind with need, his lungs burning with every breath, he drove himself into her almost savagely and heard her gasp.

Though he was half-mad with desire, he went very still. "I'm sorry, Andi. I didn't want to hurt…"

"Shh." She wrapped herself around him, all hot flesh and avid, eager mouth. Her fingers dug into his back, her nails scraping as she began to move with him, climb with him.

He couldn't stop now if he tried. His breathing was so labored he feared his lungs would surely burst. All he could see as he looked down at her were warm honey eyes locked on his. In those eyes he saw his own reflection. All he could hear was her soft breathy voice whispering his name.

For a moment he trembled on the very brink, hoping to draw out the moment of mating. Then he was moving with her, climbing, unable to stop the rollercoaster ride that had their hearts pumping, their blood rushing through their veins. Together they reached the crest and shattered into millions of tiny pieces before drifting slowly back to earth.

Andi's eyes fluttered open and she found Donovan staring down at her.

"Sorry." He touched a hand to her cheek. "I didn't mean to be so rough."

"I'm fine." She could see the look of doubt in his eyes and closed a hand over his. "Really."

"Yes, you are." He leaned down to brush a kiss over her lips. "You're better than fine. You're absolutely incredible."

"You're pretty incredible yourself. That was—" she shook her head from side to side, as though unable to believe what they'd just shared "—amazing."

"Am I too heavy?"

She shook her head.

"I have to be. I'm pressing you into the ground."

He rolled to one side, drawing her into the circle of his arms. "Are you cold?"

"After that?" She managed a laugh. "I may never cool off."

"Sorry about the grass." He glanced over at their clothes, strewn around them like discarded rags. "I guess I should have thought about bringing a blanket. But one touch of you and I lost my mind."

"Do you do that often?"

He seemed fascinated with the dark hair that framed her face. He twirled a strand around and around his finger while staring into those big liquid eyes. "As a matter of fact, I pride myself on having a reputation for being cool under fire. But this was a new experience. Like being dropped from a plane onto a bleak glacier one minute, only to find myself on a lush island paradise with the most beautiful forbidden creature on the planet." He drew her close and covered her lips with his, lingering over her mouth until they were both sighing.

When they finally came up for air, he ran a finger down the length of her throat to her breast. "Are you in a hurry to go inside?"

"Not especially. Why do you ask?"

He lowered his head, circling his tongue around one breast, then the other, until she moaned with pleasure. Against her warm flesh he murmured, "I can't let you go yet. I want you again, Andi. Here. Now."

She tried to hide her stunned reaction. "Can we? Again?"

His smile was potently male. "I can if you can."

Returning his smile, she arched herself toward him, needing the press of his body on hers. "Why, Donovan Lassiter, you're just full of surprises."

"You want surprises?" He chuckled, sending a series of tremors along her spine. "I haven't even begun yet, Ms. Brady."

They rolled together in the cool, damp grass, laughing like carefree children.

Chapter 11

Andi sat up in the dark. It took her a moment to get her bearings. Sometime in the night they had left the fragrant allure of the rose arbor for the shelter of the house, where they'd made it as far as the sofa before falling once more into each other's arms.

Donovan had proven to be the most amazing lover. In his arms she was able to forget the past. The pain. The turmoil.

In the three days that he was away she'd gone through so many changes. At first she'd experienced a sense of relief. For the first time since coming here, she had time to breathe, to think things through without the emotional roller coaster she was on each time she looked at him. But as the days wore on, she'd begun to worry that something terrible had happened to him. That was when she'd accepted the fact that, despite all the arguments to the contrary, she wanted him in her life. Though it shamed her to admit it, even to herself, this strange, dark loner had completely taken over her life and the lives of her children.

They ought to be all wrong for each other. He was moody, careless and far too wild. She was sane and sensible and, until this past year, the epitome of a suburban soccer mom. But there was no denying that when he'd left, she and her children had been under a dark cloud. And now that he was back, she felt unbelievably, gloriously happy.

She glanced at the shadowy figure standing by the window, naked to the waist, wearing only the pants he'd hastily pulled on.

It occurred to her that the night suited him. Dark. Brooding. Secretive. "Donovan? Is something wrong?"

His head came up sharply. He glanced over his shoulder. "Sorry. I didn't mean to wake you, Andi. Go back to sleep."

Instead of doing as he asked, she walked over to him and wrapped her arms around his waist, pressing her lips to his back. "This night has been wonderful."

"For me, too." He closed his hands over hers and continued to stare out into the darkness, unable to shake the feeling that he was being watched. It irritated him that even here in this sleepy little countryside, his demons continued to intrude. "I was standing here thinking about all the twists and turns my life has taken."

"Regrets?" She held her breath, waiting for his reply.

"Plenty. I don't think it's possible to live without making mistakes." He gave a mirthless laugh. "I've made more than most. But we don't get the chance to do things over. We just have to learn from past mistakes and move on."

"And are you—" she swallowed, wondering if her heart would ever resume beating "—ready to move on now?"

Something in her tone alerted him to her fear. He turned and drew her into the circle of his arms. "I wish I could tell you. I just don't have any answers. And that's not like me. I feel like I'm at some sort of crossroads in my life."

She lifted her head, trying to see his eyes in the darkness. "I don't understand."

He pressed his mouth to a tangle of hair at her

temple. "I'm not sure I do, either. My whole life seems to have been defined by my father's death. In that moment, everything changed."

"Were you angry and defiant, like Cory?"

He sighed. "Every time I look at him, I see myself. I stopped being comfortable with the familiar things in my life and did everything I could to make myself and everyone around me uncomfortable. I took crazy risks. I hurt the people who loved me." His voice lowered. "When I first met Cory, I recognized those same things in him. But I don't know how to help him, because I don't even know how to help myself."

"You've helped him just by being here. By listening to him and understanding. As for you, Donovan, you seem fine to me."

He framed her face with his hands. "That's because you don't really know me. If you did, you'd send me packing right this minute."

"I'd never do that." She pressed her lips to his throat and ran a trail of soft, butterfly kisses to his shoulder. "I know you don't like to be tied down. But don't leave me just yet, Donovan." She stood on tiptoe and found his mouth with hers. "Please don't go."

He groaned and took the kiss deeper. Against her lips he muttered, "I couldn't if I wanted to. I think you're some kind of witch. Ever since I met you, I've been under the most amazing spell.''

''If this is a spell, it's been cast over both of us.'' She opened herself to him, pouring all her heart and soul into the kiss.

''You make me weak, Andi. So weak.'' On a sigh he lifted her and carried her to the sofa.

Then there were no more words as they once again lost themselves in each other.

It wasn't yet morning, and the two lovers had spent hours in each other's arms.

Andi ran a hand along the raised scar that ran from Donovan's shoulder to his waist and felt him flinch. Against his lips she whispered, ''I've been meaning to ask you what this is.''

''Just an old wound.''

''Where did it happen?''

He stretched out his long legs and tucked his hands behind his head. ''A place with no name.''

She couldn't help smiling. He was so secretive. She curled up against him. ''What were you doing in this place with no name?''

''Infiltrating a band of international terrorists.''

Her smile faded. Whenever he talked about his past, it was so matter-of-fact. As though everyone had lived that sort of soldier-of-fortune lifestyle. "Why would you do such a thing?"

"It was my assignment. I never questioned where I was being sent. That time I almost got away with the charade, but I was found out."

"What did they do to you when they found out you weren't one of them?"

"They tortured and killed me."

She shot him a puzzled frown. "You mean they tried to."

"I mean they believe to this day that they did." His tone was patient. "You don't want to know the details. But when they were finished with me, one of their comrades examined me and declared me dead. They dumped my body in the desert. And if they hadn't left me alone in the middle of a sand dune, I'd have never been able to make my way back to safety."

"Did you deliberately play dead?"

He gave a rumble of unexpected laughter. "Sweetheart, that wasn't playacting. I was more dead than alive. And very, very lucky."

"You call that lucky?"

"I consider myself fortunate that they think they killed me. Otherwise they certainly wouldn't have stopped until they'd finished the job."

She was shaking her head in disbelief. "Why would anyone want to do the things you've done?"

"I ask myself that sometimes, in the dark of the night."

"Do you ever give yourself an answer?"

He grinned. "Not yet. But maybe one day it'll come to me."

He swung his legs over the edge of the sofa and began to dress in the predawn darkness.

She sat up with a look of alarm. "What are you doing?"

"Leaving. I think it's best if I'm gone before the kids wake up." He turned and gathered her close to press a kiss to her mouth. Just a kiss. But she felt the tremors all through her body.

As he released her she couldn't help shivering. He'd made her no promises. She'd asked for none. But she couldn't ignore the fear that ripped through her.

She watched him walk across the room. Each step away tore at her heart. She couldn't keep from calling out, "Donovan?"

He paused.

"Are you…sorry about last night?"

"Sorry? Is that what you think?" He turned and strode across the room before dropping to his knees beside the sofa. Without warning he gathered her into his arms and kissed her with a fierceness that had them both gasping.

When he could finally find the strength to release her, he held her a little away. "Never think such a thing, Andi. You're the best thing that has ever happened in my life. But I'm not about to forget that you have two little kids who are scared and confused and in pain. I think I need to tread very carefully here, so I don't add to their pain." He touched a hand to her cheek and felt another quick rush of heat. "Or to yours."

Before she could say a word he got to his feet and walked resolutely out of the room. Once outside he drew in a deep draught of air.

Leaving her had been harder than he'd expected. Even now, as he climbed into his car and drove up the hill to his own place, he wanted, more than anything, to go back inside that house and love her until they were both sated. But it was a luxury he couldn't afford right now. Perhaps, he thought with a frown, it was one he would never be able to allow himself.

Donovan spent the morning at his computer. As he scrolled through the file on the Adam Brady case, he began highlighting all the facts that pointed to Adam's guilt, putting them in one column. Then he turned to all the questionable items that might prove otherwise and placed them in another column.

Now that he'd returned from D.C. with some answers, he was no longer convinced in his own mind of Adam's guilt.

Frowning, he sat back, playing devil's advocate. Was he honestly unconvinced of that, or was it because he had become intimately involved with Andi? If Donovan should prove Adam's innocence, he would earn points not only with Andi, but with her children, as well. If, on the other hand, he should prove Adam Brady guilty, he risked damaging the people who were beginning to mean so much to him. There was so much more riding on this now. In the beginning, it had been merely a favor to an old friend. Now it had become strictly personal.

Annoyed with the direction of his thoughts he shut down the file and decided to e-mail his Washington connection with one more request. When he went on-line, he was surprised to find an e-mail waiting. The sender wasn't a name he recognized. When he opened the post the words filled the screen.

BACK OFF RIGHT NOW OR YOU'LL NEVER SEE BRADY'S KIDS ALIVE.

Donovan felt his blood freeze in his veins.

With a muttered oath he picked up the phone and dialed Andi's number. As always, whenever he'd felt the first hint of danger, his mind sharpened, his senses went on full alert.

With each ring of the phone, he felt the focus grow.

He was out the door and running to his car, the cell phone still clutched in his hand and still ringing. His tires spewed gravel as he raced down the hill and came to a screeching halt beside Andi's van.

The sight of her kneeling in a flower bed had him running full tilt across the lawn toward her.

"Donovan?" Her smile bloomed. "I was just thinking about—" As he drew close she could see the look in his eyes. "What's wrong?"

"Where are the kids?"

"What do you mean? Aren't they with you?" She was on her feet, brushing the dirt from her hands on the legs of her pants. "They asked if they could walk up to your house. I told them they could."

Seeing the look of panic coming into her eyes he grabbed her roughly by the shoulders. "Take a deep breath and think. Did you see anybody drive past here?"

She started to shake her head, then stopped. "Only a delivery truck."

"How long ago did it go by?"

"Right after Cory and Taylor left for your place. About an hour ago."

He was already dialing the phone. "Describe the truck."

"It was—" she had to choke back a sob "—white, I think. Yes. White with…yellow letters. One of those overnight delivery trucks. I thought you'd ordered something."

Donovan spoke tersely into the phone. "This is 20142 here. Terminated but still on file. This is top priority. Any report of a stolen delivery truck? Either last night or early this morning?"

He waited, hating the way Andi's face had gone ghostly white.

"Right. He's grabbed a boy of nine and a girl of five. They're wearing…" He turned to Andi, who struggled to think.

"Cory was wearing jeans and an orange T-shirt. Taylor was in pink shorts and a pink-checked shirt."

Donovan gave the description. "I'll fax their photo." In an aside he said to Andi, "Give me your most recent photo of Cory and Taylor. And an article of clothing that carries their scent." As Andi took off at a run toward the house he spoke into the phone. "Take my location. I want your best men at the mother's house, around the house and invisible until this is resolved. I want aerial surveillance. He'll ditch the truck as soon as he can, knowing it's hot. Here's my cell phone number. I'll keep it open for any report." He tucked the phone in his pocket and turned just as Andi came running across the lawn, holding out a photo of Cory and Taylor and two soiled T-shirts.

Tears streamed down her ashen cheeks. "What is this about, Donovan? Why would anyone want to harm my children?"

"Nobody's going to hurt them." He dragged her close and pressed his forehead to hers, wishing he had time to offer her the comfort she needed right now. But time was too precious. He couldn't spare even one minute.

In a tone rough with impatience he held her a little away and stared into her eyes. "Now listen to me. I know this is asking a lot, but right now you can't afford to fall apart. Cory and Taylor need you to be strong. Do you understand me?"

She nodded, struggling to shut down the sobs that had already begun. He watched her suck air into her lungs and swallow back her tears.

"Good girl." He allowed himself a quick embrace, and one slight brush of his hand along her hair before releasing her. "Now go inside and stay close to the phone. They'll need to hear their mother's voice if they should call. There will be protection here around the house. You stay inside."

She looked up at him with eyes that seemed too

big for her face. A face ravaged with terror. "What about you? Where are you going?"

He was already striding toward his car. "I'm going to bring them home. I give you my word on that."

"Lassiter?" The voice on the phone was one Donovan recognized from his days with the C.I.A.

"Yeah, Brad?"

"The truck was abandoned on a dirt road not far from you, outside the town of Prattsville. No sign of the driver or the kids. But aerial surveillance thinks they've spotted a lone man crossing a stretch of pasture not far from there."

"I want that man."

"You'll have him. If they can't land a chopper, they'll drop a couple of men who'll track him and pick him up."

"Good. Now give me the exact location of the dirt road." Donovan listened intently before saying, "Thanks, Brad." He dropped his cell phone into his shirt pocket and turned back in the opposite direction.

Fifteen minutes later, as he caught sight of the delivery truck, he was waved to the side of the road by a uniformed officer. Once Donovan flipped open his wallet and showed his identification, the officer stood to one side, allowing him to step out of his car.

Donovan moved quickly to the van, with the officer beside him. "How long do you think it's been here?"

"I was directed here by aerial, sir. That couldn't have been more than half an hour ago. After determining that the van was empty, I checked the engine. It was still warm. I was told to keep everyone away so that any evidence inside wouldn't be contaminated."

"Good work. But you saw no sign of two children?"

"No, sir."

Donovan glanced around, speaking as much to himself as to the officer. "There wouldn't have been much time for the driver to dispose of them in the woods. From the position of this van, I'd say he caught sight of the chopper overhead and made a run for it."

"Yes, sir. That's what aerial thought, too."

"Which means he'd have left two scared kids alone. So, why aren't they here?"

"He may have lost them in the woods. We have a dog and tracker on the way. Don't worry, sir. If they're in there, we'll find them."

"Good. In the meantime, I'm going ahead on my

own.'' Donovan strode to his car and retrieved the soiled T-shirts. ''Give these to the tracker.''

Like a shadow he slipped from sunlight into the damp, dark cover of the forest, his eyes straining for any sign of two frightened little children.

Chapter 12

Donovan caught sight of the orange thread snagged on a low-hanging branch. As he pulled it free he closed his hand around it. It was the first positive sign he'd found since he'd stepped into the woods fifteen minutes earlier. When he heard the gurgle of water up ahead he made his way there and paused to study two sets of small footprints along the banks of a stream.

"Good boy," he muttered. "So far you're doing everything right." Now, he thought, if only Cory could keep a cool head.

It would be so easy for two small children, on their own and running from danger, to panic and find themselves facing all sorts of trouble. The worst thing, of course, would be if they should become separated. They could end up walking in endless circles in search of each other until exhaustion overcame them.

Donovan cautioned himself not to think of that now. He needed to stay focused. But the fear that lodged in the pit of his stomach was something entirely new to him. He'd always taken every challenge as an adventure. Suddenly he was seeing in his mind's eye the faces of two children who had come to mean more to him than his own life. The thought of them alone, frightened and facing such an enormous task, had him doing something he hadn't done since he was a boy. With each step he took he found himself whispering a prayer that they would be kept safe from harm.

Andi was half crazed with worry. At first, after Donovan left, she'd been paralyzed with fear. Unable to do more than stare at the phone, willing it to ring. The silence of her house mocked her.

How often had she told the children not to slam the door? Not to shout? Now she would give anything to hear them slam the door and shout that they were home.

This couldn't be happening. Why would anyone

want to harm her children? When she'd put the question to Donovan, he had said simply that he would find them.

He would find them. She needed to believe that. If not, she wouldn't be able to stand the tension a moment longer.

Unable to sit still, she paced. With each step she prayed. Please, please, please. The word rang in her mind with an urgency that had her pausing to press a fist to her mouth to keep from sobbing.

She thought of all the times she'd seen tearful parents in the news pleading for the return of their children. Such stories always touched her mother's heart and made her react with complete sympathy. She'd always wondered how ordinary people coped with such horrifying incidents. And now it was happening to her. A nightmare from which she couldn't wake up.

The shrill ring of the telephone shattered the silence. At first all Andi could do was stare at it. Then she snatched up the receiver.

"Yes. Hello."

"Hey, Andi." Her brother's pleasant greeting had her closing her eyes. "I'm on a plane bound for London. My secretary said you called with something important. What's up?"

"Oh, Champ." Just hearing his voice had the tears starting again.

"Hey, now. Come on, honey. Tell me what's going on."

In halting tones she described what had happened.

Her brother was a man accustomed to taking charge. She could hear him speaking to someone, then his voice, shaking with frustration, came back on the line. "We won't be landing at Heathrow for another six hours. As soon as I'm through customs, I'll grab the next flight back. I won't be able to be with you until some time tomorrow, or possibly the day after that. Until then you've got to hang tough, Andi. Is Donovan Lassiter with you?"

"He's searching for Cory and Taylor."

"If anyone can find them, Donovan will." She could hear the misery in his voice. "I'm really sorry I can't be there right now, little sis. Hold on."

"I will."

"I love you, Andi."

"I know. I love you, too, Champ. Hurry home."

When the line went dead, she stood clutching the phone in both hands, fighting the rising hysteria. But she needed to be strong. For Cory's sake. For Taylor's sake. And for her own sake. She knew that if she gave in now, a floodgate would be opened, and she would weep until there were no tears left.

Donovan glanced up through the towering trees and frowned at the darkening sky, where rain clouds threatened. Just what they needed, he thought with rising impatience. A storm, to wash away what little trail he'd been able to follow.

The children had walked along the banks of the stream until it dropped off a hundred-foot cliff into a thicket far below. At first, seeing it, Donovan had feared they'd tumbled over the edge. But farther on he'd come across more prints that told him they had cautiously moved ahead.

As he picked his way through dense foliage and climbed over fallen logs, he suddenly caught sight of only one pair of footprints. From the design left in the earth by the sneakers, he knew them to be Cory's. And from the depth of the impression, he was carrying a load. Which could only mean that little Taylor had grown too tired to go on.

The boy was carrying her, probably on his back.

Even while Donovan admired Cory's courage, he felt a rising need to catch up with them soon. It was tough enough navigating a forest alone. It would be a daunting task for Cory to attempt it with the added burden of half his own body weight dragging him down.

Donovan felt an even greater sense of urgency as he stepped up his pace.

Andi stood by the phone while rain pelted the windows. The state police had alerted her that the driver of the van had been caught and was now being interrogated. But the children hadn't been with him. He claimed he'd fled the van after seeing the helicopter, leaving Cory and Taylor inside. The report stated that Donovan was in the woods, searching for them, as was a team of trackers with dogs.

"Did he say why he took my children?"

"I'm sorry, ma'am. We don't have that information yet. But we'll get back to you with a complete report as soon as we know anything."

With a heavy heart Andi watched the storm clouds rolling in. With each crash of thunder or flash of lightning, she had to choke back a sob, knowing her children were out there somewhere, alone and frightened.

Alone and frightened.

The thought tore at her heart and had her closing her eyes and whispering a prayer for courage. For Cory and Taylor. For those who tracked them. And for herself, that she could keep her nerves at bay and hold herself together.

Every tick of the clock reminded her of the passing of time. Every minute seemed like an hour. Every hour an eternity. She'd never felt so helpless. While everyone else was out searching for her children, she was forced to remain here by the phone, waiting, hoping, praying. And pacing.

She paced to the windows, peering into the gath-

ering darkness. A blinding flash of lightning
streaked across the heavens, followed by a crash of
thunder that shook the house and rattled the windows.

The storm was passing directly overhead.

Minutes later there was another jagged slice of
lightning. Andi blinked. Had she seen something
moving in the woods? Could it be the children? Or
was she just so desperate to see them, she'd imagined it?

She stepped out onto the front porch and strained
to see into the woods across the gravel road. Another
streak of lightning lit up the sky, and she was certain
she'd seen movement.

"Cory!" She shouted into the wind, but the sound
of thunder drowned out her voice.

"Cory. Taylor!" She started running, unmindful
of the torrent of rain that pelted her and the mud
that sucked at her shoes as she raced over the front
yard and across the gravel road. In a flash the men
who had been guarding her fell into step behind her.

"Andi." Donovan hurried out of the woods, his
hair plastered to his face, his clothes soaked and
flattened to his skin.

"Oh, Donovan. You didn't find them." Andi fell
into his arms, feeling her heart breaking into a million pieces.

"I lost their trail when the rain started. But

they're nearby, Andi. I know it.'' He gathered her close, wishing with all his heart that he could offer her something more than words. What she needed, what they both needed, was to see the children safe. To hold them in their arms. ''They're headed in this direction. Every indication is that…''

''Mom!''

At the sound of Cory's voice, Andi and Donovan looked up and caught sight of Cory stepping out of the woods not more than a hundred yards away. On his back was his little sister, her chubby arms wrapped around his neck in a death grip.

''Oh, my darlings.'' Andi raced across the distance that separated them and dropped to her knees in the mud. She hugged them to her heart, her tears mingling with the rain.

As she pried Taylor from her brother's back, the boy looked up at Donovan. ''I was scared.''

Taylor lifted her head from her mother's shoulder to nod. ''Me, too. Cory said it was all right to be afraid, as long as we didn't let it keep us from doing what we had to.''

Cory held up his hand. In it was the compass. ''This is what brought us home. I remembered what you said. I just stayed on course and watched for something familiar.''

Donovan stooped down and gathered the little boy against his chest, fighting a wave of such tender emotions, they threatened to break his heart. "I'm so proud of you, Cory. So proud." He looked over at the little girl. "And you, too, Taylor. You both did just fine."

He looked over to see the tears of happiness flowing down Andi's cheeks. This was, he thought, the answer to the only prayer he'd been whispering for all these miles. Now, at last, his heart could resume beating. Cory and Taylor were safely home.

Home.

It took several attempts before he managed to swallow the lump lodged in his throat. Then he helped Andi to her feet and, keeping one arm around her as she carried Taylor, held firmly to Cory's hand as they made their way back to the house.

On the porch, Andi turned to thank her guards. They had already melted into the night.

With the storm blown over, the house was blessedly silent. Andi led her children upstairs to shower and change while Donovan phoned the authorities. Once he'd alerted them that the object of their search had come home safely he firmly declared them off-limits for interrogation until they'd had time to recover from their ordeal.

Now, as he spoke by phone with his Washington contact, some of the suppressed fury seeped into his voice. "I don't care whose toes we have to step on.

I don't want to hear about rules and regulations. It may have been only a theory before, but now there isn't a doubt in my mind that what I suspected is a fact. And here's another one. He can't hide from me. He's going down. I won't rest until he pays for this."

When he hung up the phone and turned, Andi was standing in the doorway, her hand at her throat, a look of stunned surprise on her face.

"You know who did this."

He started to brush past her.

Infuriated, she stepped in front of him, hands on her hips. "You know who did this, and you don't intend to tell me?"

"There isn't time, Andi."

"Then make time."

He gave a long, slow hiss of breath. "I'll tell you when I have all the facts. Until then, you need to pack a bag for yourself and the children."

"Why should I pack a bag?"

"You can't stay here. I'm taking you someplace where you'll be safe."

He saw the fear return to her eyes and hated knowing that he was the one to put it there. With a gentleness he hadn't known he was capable of, he drew her close and brushed a kiss to her cheek. "I'm sorry to add to your burden, Andi. But trust me for a little while longer. And when the time is right, I'll tell you everything I know.''

She took a step away, tipping her head back so she could look into his eyes. She surprised him by laying a hand on his cheek.

''All right. You've bought yourself a little time. But if you think when this is over that you're going to slip away into some rain forest, or disappear without a trace, remember this. I can be as determined as you, Donovan Lassiter. I'll haunt you to your dying day, until you tell me the truth.''

He gave her an admiring look, before throwing back his head and roaring with laughter. Oh, it felt so good to be able to laugh again.

He pressed his forehead to hers. ''I like your style, Mrs. Brady. Remind me to never cross you.''

''I'm glad you understand. I may look soft, but underneath I'm hard as nails.''

''Yeah. Right.'' He gave her one of his heart-stopping smiles. ''Now go upstairs and pack. Tell the children we leave in half an hour.''

Chapter 13

It seemed to Andi that they'd been driving for hours, veering off the highway to take twisting, turning back roads, then suddenly returning to the highway after passing through a small town.

She turned to Donovan, who'd been driving in silence. "Are we lost?"

His response was a terse "No."

When she saw him glancing in the rearview mirror, she was struck by a shocking thought. "Are we being followed?"

"Not anymore."

"But we were."

He saw the look of alarm. "I lost him."

"How can you be sure?"

He reached over to lay a hand on hers. "Trust me."

"You know I do, Donovan." She sighed. "You said you were taking us someplace safe. Is this one of those government safe houses?"

He gave her a knowing smile. "In a manner of speaking."

When he returned his attention to the road, she glanced at the children in the back seat, who were busy putting together a map they'd found on the floor of Donovan's car.

"What are these little push pins for?" Cory asked.

"I started marking all the places I'd been. I never got around to finishing it."

"Wow." As the little boy studied the map, his tone turned to one of awe. "You've been just about everywhere in the whole world."

Donovan chuckled. "Not quite."

Cory followed the trail of pins with his finger. "Name a place you haven't been."

It took Donovan a few minutes before he could come up with an answer. "Fiji."

"What's Fiji?" Taylor asked.

"A string of beautiful islands in the Pacific. I'd like to go there sometime."

"Are they as pretty as Disney World?"

He couldn't help chuckling at the little girl's question. "I don't know. That's another place I've never been."

"Neither have I." The little girl met his eyes in the mirror. "My daddy promised to take me there for my birthday." Her lower lip trembled. The tension of the day, and the long drive were beginning to take their toll. "Now he'll never be here to take me."

To distract her Donovan suddenly pointed. "Look what I see."

The children stared out the window as the familiar sights of Washington, D.C., came into view.

Donovan's voice deepened with emotion. "This is something I never grow tired of seeing. Whenever I found myself in a foreign land, missing my home, I'd close my eyes and in my mind I'd see the Washington Monument, or the Lincoln Memorial, or the dome of the Capitol. I think it's one of the most beautiful places in the world."

The children sensed his emotion and watched in silence until they'd left the heart of the city behind and turned onto a street of old, stately houses.

When he pulled up the driveway and turned off the ignition, Andi glanced at him in surprise. "Where are we?"

"My childhood home." He stepped out and hurried around to open her door.

By the time he led Andi and the children up the steps, the front door was opened wide, and his entire family had spilled out onto the porch.

"Donovan." Kate Lassiter launched herself into her son's arms and gave him a fierce hug.

As soon as he was released, he was caught in a bear hug by each of his siblings.

All the while, Andi and her children stood together, looking awed and confused.

When he was able to extricate himself from their arms, Donovan turned to see Taylor hiding behind her mother's legs. He picked her up, then casually caught Cory's hand in his. "I'd like all of you to meet Andi Brady and her children, Cory and Taylor. This is my mother, Kate, my grandfather, Kieran, though we all call him Pop, and my brothers, Micah and Cameron. And the outnumbered girls in the family are my sister, Bren, and Micah's wife, Pru."

"Andi." Sensing the young woman's unease, Kate opened her arms and embraced her. "Welcome to our home."

"You're just in time for supper." Kieran winked at the little boy. "I've made Donovan's favorite."

"Spaghetti and meat sauce?" Donovan squeezed

Cory's hand. "We couldn't have planned it more perfectly."

"Come in," Kieran called, holding the door. "And make yourselves at home." As Donovan walked past him, he dropped a big hand on his shoulder and added, "You might have phoned us, boyo."

"Yeah." Donovan saw Andi and the children holding back to glance at him. "Things have been a little busy, Pop."

The old man gave a sigh before following the others inside.

Andi glanced around the big, comfortable great room, and beyond to the dining room, where the table was already set for their meal. The air was perfumed with the scent of garlic and spices and home-baked rolls.

Everyone, it seemed, was talking at once. As they talked, they moved Andi and the children along with them toward the kitchen, where six pairs of hands were instantly busy stirring, heating, pouring.

"You may as well sit." Donovan led Andi and the children toward the big trestle table. "You'll want to get out of the way of the traffic jam. When the Lassiter family is cooking, they mean business."

Here in the kitchen the smells were even stronger. Andi's mouth watered, and it occurred to her that she hadn't eaten a thing all day. Now that the crisis was over, she could admit to herself she was famished.

"I believe this calls for a celebration." Micah rummaged in a drawer for a corkscrew, then began opening a bottle of Merlot. "It's been years since Donovan visited more than once in any given year."

As he passed around stem glasses everyone took a minute to sip, before returning to their tasks.

"This is for you, lad." Kieran handed Cory a tall frosty glass of soda.

"And this is yours, lass." He winked at Taylor, and despite her shyness she managed to return a smile.

Kieran drained the pasta and arranged it on a huge platter, then ladled steaming sauce over it. "I think it's safe to say dinner is ready." He picked up the platter, and the others followed him to the dining room, each of them carrying a bowl, basket or plate of food.

Cameron had already added four more chairs at the table, and Donovan led Andi and the children to one side, facing Micah, Pru, Bren and Cameron on the other side. Kate sat at one end with Kieran at the other.

As they took their seats, they all joined hands. For a moment Cory and Taylor looked bewildered.

Then, following their mother's lead, they joined hands and stared in surprise as Kieran bowed his head and intoned in his rich brogue, "Bless this food and this family. Not only those of us gathered here, but those who are here in spirit. Bless especially our Donovan, who has returned to us along with our guests, Andi and Cory and Taylor, who share our bounty. And as always, bless Riordan, who watches over us all."

As the food was being passed around, Taylor whispered to Cory, "Is Donovan's grandpa a preacher?"

Overhearing, Kieran threw back his head and roared. "Not a preacher, lass. Just a son of the auld sod who loves to pray aloud."

Donovan winked. "He loves to hear himself talk."

"Watch it, boyo." Kieran shot him a quelling look. "Or you'll be outside shooting hoops while the rest of us devour this good food."

"What's shooting hoops?" Taylor helped herself to a hot, buttery roll and passed the basket to her mother.

"It's a peculiar form of discipline that our grandfather inflicts on us," Micah explained. "From the time we were your age, we've been sent to the backyard to work off our aggression on a basketball hoop whenever we got out of hand.''

The girl's eyes got round. "But you're big men. Does he still send you outside?"

"He does if we get out of line." Cameron was grinning. "And that includes our sister, Bren. Even though she's a congresswoman now, she isn't immune to Pop's discipline."

"Of course." Andi dropped her fork to stare at the pretty redhead across the table. "I thought you looked familiar." She turned to Donovan. "Why didn't you tell me that Congresswoman Lassiter is your sister?"

He shrugged. "You never asked. Besides, I find it a little hard to believe myself. When I went away, she was just another college babe, trying to snag the attention of all my buddies, including, I might add, your brother, Champ. Now I come home to find out she's practically running the country."

"Don't I wish." Bren laughed along with her brothers. "I'm still learning the ropes, but I'm finding it exciting and rewarding to be working in government."

"Is your job like Donovan's?" Cory asked innocently.

That had the entire family laughing.

Bren shook her head. "I'm afraid not. As a matter

of fact, Donovan has yet to tell us exactly what his work consisted of.''

"Don't hold your breath." He blew her a kiss. "I'm taking all my secrets to the grave."

Andi sat back, enjoying the interplay between Donovan and his family. There was so much warmth and laughter here. She could feel it wrapping itself around her, making her feel more relaxed than she'd felt in a very long time.

Cory looked over at Donovan. "You were right."

"About what?"

"About Pop's spaghetti being the best in the world."

Kieran looked up, his silver hair glinting in the light of the chandelier. "Donovan said that?"

"Uh-huh." The little boy saw the look that passed between Donovan and his grandfather.

Then the moment passed, and Kate was pouring tea while Bren and Pru were fetching the dessert from the kitchen. They passed around slices of rich cheesecake drizzled with raspberry sauce, and a bowl of fresh berries frosted with confectioner's sugar.

Andi nibbled a slice of cheesecake and sipped her tea. "Do all of you come together every night for dinner?"

Kate shook her head. "Once or twice a week is

more like it. We're all so busy these days. But everyone in the family knows that our door is always open.''

''And there's always good food on the stove,'' Kieran said with a twinkle in his eye.

''He ought to know.'' Donovan grinned at his grandfather. ''He's the chief cook and bottle washer.''

Andi looked around. ''You're all so lucky to have each other.''

''Indeed we are.'' Kate topped off her cup before passing the teapot to Andi.

Across the table Micah was studying his brother. ''So, were you just out for a joyride? Or was it something else that brought you here?''

Pru, who had remained quiet throughout the meal, pushed away from the table and glanced at Cory and Taylor. ''Would you two like to help me in the kitchen? I'll show you the backyard, where the Lassiter family has been shooting hoops for most of their lives.''

After glancing at their mother and seeing her nod of approval, the two children were out of their seats in a flash and following Pru from the room.

When the door closed behind them, Donovan turned to his mother. ''I was wondering if Andi and the kids could stay here for a few days.''

Kate smiled at Andi. "Of course you can. With my children growing up and moving out, we have plenty of bedrooms."

Andi was moved by the warmth of her tone. "I don't like to intrude."

"Nonsense." Kieran helped himself to the last piece of cheesecake. "It'll be good to have some of those empty rooms filled again. The house won't seem so lonely."

Donovan motioned toward the kitchen, where he could hear the children's voices raised in laughter. "Where would you like them?"

"Why not give Cory Micah's old room and put Taylor in Cameron's room. That way Andi can have Bren's room, with its own bath, and you can have your old room, Donovan."

He was already shaking his head. "I won't be staying. I…have things to see to."

Kieran pointed with his fork. "You can stay the night, boyo. There'll be time enough to do whatever you have to do tomorrow."

When he saw the hopeful look in his mother's eyes, it was on the tip of Donovan's tongue to agree. But this was too important to wait even one night. He shook his head. "Sorry, Pop. There's nothing I'd like better than to have a good night's sleep in my old room. But I have to do this."

He pushed away from the table and paused to press a hand to Andi's shoulder. Then he dropped a kiss on his mother's cheek before starting toward the kitchen. Just then Cory and Taylor walked into the dining room, their faces wreathed in smiles.

"Pru showed us the basketball hoop. And she said she'd teach us how to shoot baskets."

"Not on your life." Cameron grinned at his sister-in-law. "She'll teach you sissy shots. If anybody's going to teach you how to make baskets, it'll be me."

"Wow. Thanks." Cory turned to Donovan. "Pru showed us the tree where you used to have a tree house. Do you think you and I could build one together?"

Donovan could feel his family watching him. "That's something I'll have to think about. As soon as I get back."

"Get back?" Cory looked around. "Are we leaving?"

"I'm leaving. You're staying here, where you'll be safe." Donovan was halfway to the front door when Cory's shout pierced the silence, shocking everyone.

"No!" He darted across the room and flung himself at Donovan's legs.

Caught by surprise, Donovan reacted instinctively, turning and grabbing the boy roughly by the arms.

Despite the man's strength and size, Cory managed to free himself and began pummeling Donovan with his fists.

"Hey, now." Donovan was frowning as he held the boy a little away. "What's all this?"

"You can't go. I won't let you." To Cory's mortification, tears streamed from his eyes and down his face. He wiped at them with the backs of his hands. His tone turned pleading. "Please don't go, Donovan. If you do, I know you'll never come back."

For several moments Donovan simply stared at this little boy as the truth dawned.

He dropped to his knees and dragged Cory close, burying his face in the boy's hair. "I'm not your father, Cory. I'm not about to crash and burn."

"You don't know that. It happened before. It can happen again." The words were muffled against his shirt.

Donovan looked helplessly across the room, only to see Andi and Taylor weeping, as well. He felt his heart take several hard hits before he managed to say, "I give you my word, Cory. I'm not going to die. I'm coming back."

The boy merely shook his head and continued sobbing.

Donovan got to his feet, still holding the boy in his arms. Against his cheek he murmured, "You've had to deal with a lot of things that most kids your age haven't even thought of. I wish I could make this easier for you, Cory, but there's still too much I can't talk about. You have to just trust me. Do you think you can do that?"

"No. I don't mind trusting you, but I don't want you to go." The boy wrapped his arms around Donovan's neck as Andi picked up her daughter and walked up to stand beside them.

"Let's go outside and I'll see if I can answer a few of your questions before I go." As he turned toward the porch, Donovan was aware that his entire family was watching in silence. By the time he opened the door he could hear the whispers, and figured they were having a grand time speculating on his relationship with Andi and the children.

His relationship.

Maybe, he thought as he stepped out on the porch, they'd figure it out among themselves and let him in on it. Especially since he wasn't at all certain what their relationship really was. Or where it was headed. All he knew was that he'd willingly die rather than see any of them harmed in any way.

If that made him a fool in love, so be it.

Right now he had more important things to deal

with. He was about to give his word to Cory that he'd come back, while knowing that life, especially the reckless life he chose to lead, offered no guarantees.

Chapter 14

Andi poured herself a cup of coffee and walked to the window to watch her two children shooting hoops in the backyard. She and Donovan had sat with Cory and Taylor until they'd calmed down enough to accept the fact that he was leaving.

When he drove away, she'd felt as desperately afraid and unhappy as Cory.

In anticipation of the morning, Kieran poured coffeecake batter into a pan before setting it in the oven. Then he helped himself to the last cup of coffee and placed the empty pot in the sink.

"So. How is your brother, Champion?"

"He's doing fine. His international business is

flourishing. He's in London now, and should be on his way home tomorrow.''

''You'll be glad to see him.''

She nodded. ''There have been so many changes in my life since he saw me last.''

Kieran chose his words carefully. ''Would one of those changes happen to be Donovan?''

She could feel herself blushing. ''Is it that obvious?''

''Even a blind man could tell.'' His voice gentled. ''A word of warning, lass. Donovan's a hard man to love. He doesn't let anyone get too close.''

''I know.'' She turned to the window. ''But there's just something about him. Despite his toughness, there's such goodness in his heart. I can see the changes in my children. Taylor adores this man who can tease and laugh and make her feel safe. Cory is pinning all his hopes on Donovan.''

''How about their mother?''

She turned to the old man. ''I've lost my heart to him, Pop. I never would have believed this possible. I had a good marriage. I loved Adam. We'd built a fine life together. But with Donovan everything is different. There's this dangerous side to him that makes him so exciting.''

''Exciting, is it?'' The old man's lips thinned. ''Maybe to a woman in love. But to his family that dangerous side has caused a good deal of heartache. Have you given any thought to what it would be like to be married to a man like Donovan? Never knowing where he was. Always wondering if he was alive or dead. Or if he'd ever come back to you. There's a restlessness inside him. I've never understood it. Nor have I approved.''

Andi touched a hand to his. ''I couldn't help noticing that. You realize, of course, that Donovan notices, too.''

''If he does, he's never let it stop him from doing exactly as he pleases.''

Andi leaned against the counter and studied the handsome, weathered face. ''He told me you were a wild man in your youth. He said you were one of the toughest cops on the D.C. force. And he said you and his father had always been his heroes.''

The old man's frown faded. ''He did, did he?'' He seemed to lose himself in thought for a moment before saying, ''I'm sure I gave my family plenty of bad moments. But I knew that what I was doing was the right thing, even if it meant frightening those who loved me, and putting my own life on the line.''

As soon as the words were spoken, he arched a brow and turned to her. ''You're a sly one, Andi Brady.''

She smiled. "Now whatever do you mean by that, Pop?"

"You knew if you pushed hard enough I'd end up defending him, didn't you?"

Her smile grew. "I'm told it runs in the family. Donovan said that no matter how far away he was, or how desperate the situation, he always took comfort in the knowledge that his family loved him."

"That we do, lass." Kieran turned away and busied himself at the sink until the lump in his throat was gone. "I just hope he confronts this villain quickly and hurries back to us. We've a lot of missed time to catch up on."

Andi kept her tone casual. "Did he say where he was going?"

"Not in so many words. But I have an idea that he was going back to his place."

Andi glanced at the keys hanging in a neat row by the back door. "I know I can count on you to keep my children safe, Pop."

"Of course. Didn't I give my word to Donovan?" He turned and saw the direction of her gaze. "You'd be wise not to meddle in his business, lass."

"I never said I was wise, Pop. After all, I'm a woman in love with a man who lives on the edge. And that's just about the most foolish thing I know.'' She took in a deep breath. ''Would you mind if I borrowed your car?''

He sighed. ''The third key ring from the left. There's a full tank of gas.''

She walked up to him and pressed a kiss to his leathery cheek. ''You're a softie.''

''Soft in the head, you mean. You tell my grandson he's a fool if he doesn't appreciate you.''

''I'll do that.'' She snatched up the keys and hurried out the door, before she had time to think about what she was about to do. For if she spent even a minute thinking this through, she'd lose her courage and give it up entirely.

But as she'd admitted to Kieran, there was just something about being with Donovan Lassiter that made her feel reckless and bold.

Whatever he was facing, at least this time he wouldn't face it alone.

Donovan left his car in a stand of trees and started up the gravel road on foot, his senses alert to anything out of the ordinary. He moved with the sureness of one who'd spent a lifetime staring down unknown peril. As he passed the rental house, he thought about the night he'd spent lying in Andi's arms. She'd become very special to him. As had her children. Still, the thought of a lifetime commitment had him backing off. He'd spent so many years without roots, without permanence in his life. What gave him the right to think he should inflict himself on three people who had already had their lives shattered by violent death? He would probably be the worst thing that could happen to them. Still, the thought was tempting.

As he approached his darkened house at the top of the hill he paused, listening.

The night seemed almost too silent. No birds cried. No insects chirped. Even the breeze had died down, so that the leaves in the trees were as still, as motionless, as death.

He made a complete turn around the house until, satisfied, he walked up the steps of the porch and opened the front door. He didn't flick on the lights, choosing instead to cross the room in darkness. He paused at the wall of shelves to reach for the night binoculars, then walked to the window and stared out into the darkness.

"You're looking in the wrong place, Lassiter." A man's voice came from across the room. "I'm right here behind you."

Donovan didn't bother to turn. "I just wanted to make sure you were alone."

"You don't sound surprised to see me here."

"No more surprised than you are to see me." He

did turn then, and lowered the binoculars. "You knew, when you grabbed Adam's children, that I'd be back to finish this."

"I was counting on it." The man touched a hand to the wall switch, flooding the room with light. In his hand was a gun, aimed directly at Donovan's chest. "I'd been so careful to leave no loose ends. I was home free. And then you had to come along and muddy the water. Which means, of course, that you'll now have to drown in it."

Donovan studied the man, whose blond hair and unlined face made him completely unrecognizable from his photograph. "Quite an improvement over the old Neil Summerville. Plastic surgery?"

The lips smiled, though the eyes remained cold. "Amazing what enough money can buy today. A new face. Hair implants. A brand-new identity." His tone sharpened. "Why couldn't you have left it alone?"

"I was doing a favor for an old college friend."

"Champion Mackenzie. In all my research on Adam Brady, I never came across the fact that his brother-in-law had once roomed in college with a government spy. If I had, I'd have figured a way to have Mackenzie on that plane with him."

"A loose end." Donovan kept his voice bland. "So, Neil, what excuse did you give Adam for missing the flight?"

"I met him at the plane and told him I'd snagged a multimillion-dollar investor who wanted to meet with me that morning. I suggested that he go ahead to Chicago without me."

"Where did you hide the explosives?"

Neil smiled. "I suppose, in your line of work, you have a need for all the little details."

"That's right. So indulge me."

"In a satchel under the pilot's seat. I wasn't taking any chances on the pilot surviving long enough to bail out and possibly swim to shore."

"You knew the explosion would happen over water?"

"Of course. I planned the timer that way, so they would never be able to recover more than bits and pieces of the plane or the bodies."

"I suppose you also planted some of your own belongings, so there'd be no question that you'd been aboard?"

"Exactly." Neil smiled. "You see, Lassiter? We think alike. You'd make a formidable criminal."

"So I've been told." Donovan started to set the binoculars on a nearby table, and Summerville jumped back before taking careful aim with his pistol.

Donovan merely smiled. "Just tired of holding these."

"You make another move, I'll blow you apart where you stand."

Donovan's smile widened. "Isn't that why you came here?"

"That's right. After I eliminate this loose end, I'll go back to my new life, with my new lover and a portfolio worth millions."

"You had this planned from the beginning, didn't you, Neil? That's why you invited Adam to join your firm. So you could set him up for the fall."

"Here was a guy with some of the best money connections in the country, and he was miserably unhappy with the family business. Add to that the fact that he was more concerned with being a doting husband and father than he was with all the little details of his investment clients, and you had a man born to be the perfect patsy."

His voice lowered. "Now you, on the other hand, looked completely invulnerable. All my sources said that Donovan Lassiter had no weaknesses. I couldn't figure out how to get you to back off this investigation. And then, when I followed you home from D.C., I found your Achilles' heel. The lovely widow Brady and her two kids."

Donovan thought about that feeling he'd had of being watched. It was the first time he'd ignored his instinct to investigate further. But being with Andi had clouded his mind. "Would you have killed them?"

Neil threw back his head and laughed. "Without a moment's hesitation." He lifted the gun and took careful aim. "The same way I'm about to kill you, Lassiter."

Both men looked up when headlights swung up the lane and a car came to a lurching stop. A door slammed, and hurried footsteps signaled the approach of someone racing across the porch.

The door was pushed open, and Andi paused to catch her breath. As she did she let out a sigh. "Oh, Donovan. I was so afraid I'd be too—"

She stopped when she caught sight of the stranger across the room. Her gaze flew to the gun in his hand, then back to Donovan. "Is this the man who kidnapped my children?"

"Little fool." The man turned slightly, aiming the gun at her. "You couldn't leave well enough alone, could you? Now your two brats are going to be orphans."

Her eyes widened. "I know that voice. But it doesn't match the face and—"

"Plastic surgery." Though Donovan hadn't moved a muscle, his mind had already raced ahead, looking for a way to deflect Summerville's attention away from Andi and back to him. "Neil was tired of his old life. And apparently tired of his old wife, as well.''

The man shrugged. "It pained me to know that, as my widow and legal heir, she would get the house and the business, such as it is. But now I'm free to live my life as I please.''

"What about your children?'' Andi's voice betrayed her depth of her shock and pain. "They're grieving for a dead father, while you're…enjoying this so-called freedom.''

"It couldn't be helped. Not if I was going to pull this off and start with a clean slate.''

Donovan turned to Andi, hoping to keep the conversation going. "With the authorities believing Neil was dead along with Adam, he achieved two things. The investigation into his business was halted. And with no one looking for him, he's free to spend the millions he stole from Adam's clients, without having to flee the country.''

"You see, Lassiter, we do think alike.'' Neil's tone hardened. "That's why I knew I had to eliminate you. Otherwise, you'd have dug up all my skeletons.''

Andi shook her head. "How did you know that Donovan was investigating the crash?''

"Being rich gives me a few added benefits. Enough money to the right people, and I get a message whenever someone goes into the Brady-Summerville files. It would take someone with top government clearance to dig as deeply as Lassiter did.''

''But I don't understand why you took my children.''

''When I found out who was doing the digging, I made it my business to learn all I could about Donovan Lassiter. With his record, I realized that he wasn't going to give up until he got to the truth. Something I couldn't allow. So I followed him home, hoping to put an end to him that night. Only he didn't go home, Mrs. Brady. He went to your bed.'' Summerville sneered. ''That's when the light went on. I realized the spy had just revealed a weakness. Knowing his background, I figured he'd come after the kids, and I'd eliminate him and them, along with the ex-con I'd hired to drive the truck. It was all so simple, and was going as planned, until the stupid con panicked at the first sign of a police helicopter and ruined all my plans.''

He took careful aim with the gun. ''Now I'll just have to improvise.''

Andi felt her heart contract.

She turned to Donovan. ''Neil is right. Because of my meddling, my children will now be forced to grieve the loss of both their parents. It's breaking my heart to know I've let them down. But I'm not sorry I'm here with you, Donovan."

"Andi, don't…"

She held up a hand to stop him. "If these are our last minutes alive, I need to tell you this. These past weeks have been so amazing. I'll always be grateful to my brother for bringing you into my life. I appreciate all you did for us. Not just because you proved Adam's innocence, but also for what you did for my children. Cory was hurt and angry and defiant. He was lost, and you helped him find himself. And Taylor." Andi felt tears fill her eyes and blinked furiously. She wasn't about to allow any tears to mar her last words. "She was so shy and frightened. And thanks to you, she's begun to trust again. As for me." She felt her lower lip quivering and bit down hard. "I never thought I could feel this way again. My heart is so filled with love. You did that, Donovan. And for that, I'm so grateful. If I have to die, I'm glad you're here with me to give me the courage I need."

He shook his head. "You don't need anyone to give you courage, Andi. You're the bravest woman I've ever known."

"This is all very touching." Neil Summerville's voice had them turning toward him as he leveled the gun. "Now it's time to say goodbye."

Chapter 15

"You don't want to do that, Neil." Donovan moved very deliberately, placing himself in front of Andi.

"Always the hero, aren't you, Lassiter." The gunman gave a chilling laugh. "But you won't be able to play hero once you're dead."

"You're the one who's dead, Neil." Donovan touched a hand to his chest. "I'm wearing a wire. Everything you've said has been recorded for posterity."

"You're lying." But even as Neil shook his head in denial, his face drained of color.

He strode forward and reached a hand to Donovan's shirt. That was all the distraction Donovan needed. His fist shot out, catching Neil in the midsection. As the gun clattered to the floor, Donovan's fist connected with Neil's jaw, sending him reeling backward, slamming against the wall.

He paused to clear his vision, then lunged forward, ramming his head into Donovan's chest with enough force to send them both tumbling to the floor, where they rolled around and around, grunting with pain each time another blow landed.

Neil Summerville was in excellent shape. His workouts with a personal trainer were paying off. Though most men would be winded, he seemed to grow stronger with each exchange of blows. But even he was no match for the kind of street fighting Donovan had mastered. When Donovan drove him back against the floor under a barrage of fists, Neil could feel his strength ebbing. He reached out blindly until his hand closed around the cold metal of his gun.

"Had enough?" Donovan lifted a fist, intent upon finishing the job.

Neil raised his hand and took aim. "Yeah, Lassiter. I've had enough. And so have you."

"No!" Andi's shout seemed to echo around the room at the same moment that the shot roared like thunder.

Neil gave a hiss of pain and slumped to the floor. Broken glass rained down on him.

Donovan looked up to see Andi holding tightly to what was left of his binoculars.

Blood streamed down the front of his shirt, and she couldn't look away. "Oh no." She bit back a cry. "Donovan, you've been hit. Oh, my God, you're bleeding."

He shook his head. "He had a lousy aim, thanks to your little distraction. This is just a bloody nose." His eye was beginning to swell almost shut, and her image was beginning to fade a bit. Still he managed to grin up at her. "Couldn't you have found something else to use on him? Do you know what those binoculars cost Uncle Sam?"

They slipped from her fingers as she dropped to her knees beside him to cradle his face in her hands. "Oh, Donovan. My poor, sweet Donovan."

The door burst open and half a dozen men came streaming inside, all of them holding guns.

Andi let out a scream until one of them had the presence of mind to hold out a badge.

"Government agents, ma'am." The tall, rangy man stood looking down at Donovan.

"What the hell took you so long?" Donovan thought about getting up, but it felt too good here

in Andi's arms. He figured he'd stay put a minute
or two more until he'd caught his breath.

"Sorry, Donovan. It was all going well until
Wonder Woman came flying in. She sort of caught
us all by surprise."

"Wonder Woman?" Andi didn't know whether
to feel flattered or insulted. "Are you talking about
me?"

"We were hiding out in the woods, ma'am. When
you raced by us, we weren't sure what to do about
you. As far as we could tell, you weren't part of the
scenario."

He watched as Neil Summerville was cuffed and
hauled outside. "So we decided to stick with the
script. We kept on listening and taping, and figured
we'd move in when things got too tense." He
grinned at Donovan. "But one minute we were getting the proof we needed, and the next we thought
we'd crossed our wires and had picked up a soap
opera."

At Donovan's questioning look he said, "Washington's going to love hearing how much the lady
loves you."

Andi's cheeks turned several shades of red. The
thought of all these strangers listening to her heart-
felt declaration had her moaning with embarrass-
ment.

The agent took no notice. "Glad you finally managed to subdue our guy." He nodded toward the binoculars. "Too bad about the equipment."

"Yeah. But it was sacrificed for a good cause."

"You want us to call for a medic, Lassiter?" someone shouted.

Donovan shook his head. "As far as I can tell, I've just got a few bumps and bruises."

"And the lady?"

Donovan lifted a hand to Andi's cheek and gave her one of those heart-stopping grins. "Wonder Woman's just fine, too. In fact, better than fine. She saved my hide."

"Don't know why she'd bother. Your hide's tough enough to withstand guided missiles." The man patted his pocket. "We've got all we need to put Neil Summerville away for life. The press is going to have a field day with this information."

Donovan nodded. "Just so they clear Adam Brady's name."

He lay quietly, his head in Andi's lap, as men moved around the room, snapping photographs, tagging evidence. All the while they engaged in teasing patter, as though this sort of thing happened every day.

When they were finally alone Andi closed her eyes a moment, trying to take it all in. "My children have their good name back. Their friends, their relatives will know that Adam was innocent.''

"That's right." Donovan shifted, until he was sitting beside her. "Why the hell did you risk everything to drive up here?''

She smiled. "Why did you?''

"It's my job, Andi.''

She shook her head. "I don't believe you. I think there was much more to this than simply doing your job.''

He shrugged. "Maybe. But that doesn't explain why you put yourself in harm's way.''

"I realized that I didn't want you to face whatever it was you were facing, alone. You've been doing that for too long, Donovan.''

He was staring at her with that strange intensity that always had her throat going dry. Without a word he got to his feet, before holding out a hand and helping her up.

When she was standing beside him, he smoothed the hair from her cheek before brushing his lips over hers. "I'd better get you back. It's late. Everyone will be worried.''

He draped an arm around her shoulders and led her toward his car. Seeing his grandfather's car parked beside it, he arched a brow. "Does Pop know you took this?''

She lifted her chin. "I didn't take it without permission. He gave me his keys."

"Wow." He helped her into his car, then walked around and slid behind the wheel. "Pop never lets anyone drive his car. Not even my mother. You must have made some kind of impression on him."

She leaned her head back and closed her eyes. A while later she glanced over, studying Donovan's profile as though through new eyes. Where she'd once seen defiance, she now saw strength. Where she'd once seen a man of mystery, she now saw a man of courage. But she'd been right about one thing. Donovan Lassiter was a loner. Nothing had changed that. He'd faced down Neil Summerville alone, without regard for his own safety, in order to get what he needed for a conviction.

She ought to feel on top of the world. Instead, she was feeling as though she carried the weight of the world on her shoulders. She was, she realized, hopelessly, helplessly in love with a man who, though he might return her feelings, would never be tied down. It was time to face the truth. If she truly loved him, she had to be willing to let him go.

"Mama." When Andi and Donovan arrived at the Lassiter home, Taylor hurled herself into her mother's arms. "Daddy's face was on television."

"On the news," Cory shouted, racing up behind his sister.

He paused in midstride when he caught sight of Donovan's bruised cheek and swollen eye. "You look worse than I did when I got in a fight after school."

"Yeah?" Donovan merely grinned at him and tousled his hair.

"Come on, Mama." Taylor had her mother by the hand and was leading her into the great room, where the rest of the Lassiter family had gathered around the TV.

"Have you heard the news?" Cameron looked up, then did a double take when he saw Donovan. "Looking good, bro."

"You ought to see the other guy." Donovan managed a smile as he sank down into an overstuffed chair and listened to the news anchor announce that Adam Brady's plane had been sabotaged, and the death of Neil Summerville faked in order to cover his theft of millions of dollars.

"I knew my dad never stole that money." Needing to be close, Cory balanced himself on the arm of Donovan's chair.

When a live shot of Neil Summerville being arraigned came on the screen, Cory turned to Donovan. "He looks like he's been in a fight, too."

"You think so?" Donovan continued watching the television. But he could feel Cory studying him.

"Was he the other guy?"

Donovan merely winked at him.

Taylor, sitting on her mother's lap, turned her head. "Does this mean we can go back home now, Mama?"

"I don't see why not. All your old friends will believe you now. And your schoolmates won't have anything to tease you about anymore."

"But where's our home now?" Cory looked as unhappy as he had the first day Donovan had met him. "In the city or in the country?"

Andi glanced at Donovan, but it was impossible to read anything in his shuttered expression. She gave a sigh. "We agreed that we'd just stay for the summer, until it was time for school to start."

"Don't they have any schools in the country?"

"Of course they do, Cory, but…"

Andi was distracted when Taylor climbed down from her lap and walked over to Donovan. Like her mother she framed his big face with her pudgy little hands. She seemed fascinated with his swollen eye and bloody lip. "Does it hurt?"

"Not much."

She was so serious. "If you'd like, Mama and I could take care of you until it's all better."

He experienced a quick tug on his heart. "Thank you, Taylor. That's…very generous of you. But I think your mama's got her hands full already."

"No, she doesn't." Cory stood with his hands fisted at his sides. "She likes having you around. I can tell. And so do—" he stared down at the floor "—so do I."

"Me, too," Taylor said with a nod of her little head.

"Let me get this straight." Donovan reached over and tilted Cory's face up. "Are you saying you want me around? All the time?"

The boy met his eyes. "I know you're used to being alone, but Taylor and I wouldn't bother you much."

"That's right. Except when we're chasing my woodchuck." The little girl scrambled to stand beside her brother, closing her hand in his for courage.

If they were going to take a stand, they'd take it together.

"I told you earlier, Cory. I'm not your father." Donovan was so intent upon choosing the right words, he failed to notice Andi slip from the room, blinking back tears.

Cory swallowed back his disappointment. "I know you're not my dad. But I thought…I was hoping…"

Donovan dropped to his knees in front of the boy and girl. "I can't ever take the place of your father. But I'd be proud and honored to marry your mom if she'd have me, and to be the best stepfather I could be. But only if that's what the two of you want, as well."

Cory's eyes lit. "I wouldn't mind if you married my mom."

Taylor was nodding. "Then we could be like a family again."

"That would mean you'd have to become part of my family, too." Donovan glanced around the room to see his entire family watchful and silent. His sister Bren's jaw had dropped. Cameron was grinning like a fool. Micah and Pru were holding hands and smiling.

"Wow. That's neat." Cory looked over at the smiling, handsome men who all resembled the man he'd begun to worship. "Would they be my aunts and uncles and grandparents and stuff?"

"They would. And Pop would be your great-grandfather." Donovan was startled to see Kieran wipe a tear from his eye before walking deliberately toward him.

"There's something I need to say, boyo."

Donovan got to his feet, prepared to face whatever complaint the old man was about to make. "Sorry, Pop. I know I didn't have any right—"

"Enough of that now." Kieran cleared his throat. "I know you can't talk about what you've done for all these years. But I'm so…" He cursed himself for the way his voice shook. "I'm so glad you've come home. You've put the light back in your mother's eyes. And you've made this old man so proud of you."

He caught his grandson in a fierce bear hug. Soon the two men were surrounded by the rest of their family, who took turns embracing first Donovan, then Kieran, before breaking into shouts and cheers.

It was, Donovan realized, the homecoming he'd always envisioned. A little late. But having Andi and the children here to share it made it even better.

Andi.

He glanced around and realized she was missing from the celebration. While the others milled about, laughing and talking in almost giddy tones, Andi was nowhere to be seen.

He turned to his family. "Has anyone seen Andi?"

Kate pointed. "I saw her heading out back to shoot some hoops."

Cory looked puzzled. "Mom doesn't play basketball, Donovan. What does it mean?"

"It means your mother has some rather deeply rooted aggression she needs to resolve. Or maybe I should say we need to resolve." Donovan kissed Taylor's cheek, then turned to Cory. "You and your sister stay here. I think this calls for some tactical maneuvers."

"Yes, sir."

The children watched as he walked from the room. As soon as he was gone, the entire Lassiter family gathered around Cory and Taylor and led them toward the kitchen windows overlooking the backyard, where they could watch and listen.

Donovan tucked his hands in his back pockets as Andi tossed the ball toward the basket. It fell far short, and she charged forward to retrieve it. Ignoring him, she tossed it again and missed.

"I don't think basketball's your game."

She shot him a killing look and tried again. This time the ball rimmed the basket before rolling away. With a hiss of annoyance she charged forward once again and caught it, before giving a furious toss.

When it sailed through the hoop, Donovan chuckled. "Okay. Maybe it isn't your game, but at least you're getting the hang of it. Still, I think I like playing baseball with you better."

"I'm not in the mood for jokes. Leave me alone, Donovan. I came out here to be by myself."

"It's not all it's cracked up to be."

She turned, clutching the ball to her chest. "What isn't?"

"Being alone. I ought to know. I'm the expert on it."

She studied him a moment before dribbling the ball and running up to toss it in for another basket.

"Maybe I was wrong." When she turned he was directly behind her. "Maybe this is your game."

"Wrong. Games aren't my thing." She thrust the basketball against his chest and started away.

He tossed the ball aside and grabbed her arm, turning her to face him. "And relationships aren't mine."

She shrugged off his hands. Before she could open her mouth to protest, he added, "But I'm willing to learn."

His words stopped her cold. "What are you saying, Donovan?"

"What I never thought I'd say to any woman. I'm in love with your kids, Andi."

"Right. So much so that you don't want to be their father."

"Is that what you think?" He smiled as understanding dawned. "I get it. You heard me say I wasn't their father, and then you left, before I told them how proud I would be if they were mine."

"You said that?"

"Yeah. Right after admitting that I'm desperately in love with their mother."

"You're—" She blinked. "When did you come to this conclusion?"

"It took me a while. Probably a full minute after I met you. But I'm not sure when lust turned to something deeper. Maybe when I tasted your potato salad." His smile faded. "Or maybe when Summerville had the kids snatched. I was afraid my heart would never be the same. And when you turned into Wonder Woman and came charging up to rescue me, I knew I'd met my perfect match."

"So." She gave him a long, slow look. "What do you intend to do about this?"

He shrugged. "That's up to you. You need to know that I'm not an easy man to live with. I'm moody. I can spend hours at my computer, lost in my work. What's worse, I'm a slob."

"I'm compulsively neat. I'm happiest when I have a list of chores I can cross off when they're completed every day." She sighed. "Now tell me something I don't know."

He tensed. "All right. Time for some honesty here." He stared into her eyes, willing her to understand. "There are dark places inside me that you'll never understand, Andi. Places you can never go."

He saw the look of concern in her eyes and wondered if his heart might stop beating entirely.

Slowly she reached a hand to his face. "I'll miss you when you pull away from me. But I'll try to be patient until you come out of the darkness."

He took in a long, deep breath. "You're an amazing woman, Andi Brady." He had been, he realized, scared to death at the thought of his honesty driving her away.

A smile curved his mouth. "I'm thinking that we could keep our place in the country, and maybe buy a second house around here, so the kids could have the best of both worlds. You know. Aunts and uncles. Grandparents. A big noisy family. What do you think?"

She took a step back. "Are you talking about a long-term commitment here?"

"Well, yes. I was thinking—" he swallowed "—marriage."

"Marriage. And you're busy making plans without saying the words?"

"What words?"

Her lips turned into a pout. "The words a man uses when he wants to ask a woman to share his life."

"Oh." He grinned. "Those words. Andi, would you…"

She was already shaking her head. "I think you

should get down on your knees. It's so much more romantic.''

"You want romance? Find yourself a movie star.'' Without warning he grabbed her by the upper arms and hauled her against him, covering her mouth with his in a kiss that curled her toes and sent heat rushing through her veins. Then he took it deeper, until she was breathless and clinging. "I love you, Andi Brady, more than life itself.'' He spoke the words inside her mouth and she felt them all the way to her heart. "I want to grow old with you.'' He kissed her cheek, her forehead, the tip of her nose. "I want to carry your daughter on my shoulders to her brother's soccer games. I want to build a tree house in the woods, and spend nights up there with Cory and Taylor. I want your beautiful face to be the first thing I see every morning when I wake and the last I see every night. For as long as I live.''

"Oh, Donovan.'' She wrapped her arms around his neck, knowing he'd just described heaven. "I can't think of anything that would make me happier than to spend the rest of my life with you.''

She held on tightly as he lifted her off her feet and swung her around and around. By the time he set her down she was giddy as a child.

It was then that they heard the sound of cheering

and looked up to see their family at the windows, laughing and waving. Cory and Taylor were jumping up and down with excitement.

Donovan drew her close. "I forgot what a pack of busybodies my family can be. Let's say we pack up the kids and head on back to the woods."

"Are you serious? It'll be past midnight before we get there."

"Yeah." He gave her that heart-stopping smile that she'd come to love. "We'll tuck the kids in and we'll have hours of privacy before they wake up."

She was laughing. "I love the way you think."

Just then Cory and Taylor rushed out the door and down the steps, unable to contain their excitement any longer.

"If we're getting married," Taylor shouted, "are we going on a honeymoon?"

Cory's eyes lit. "Yeah. Maybe someplace exotic. Like...Fiji."

Donovan winked at Taylor. "I was thinking something more adventurous. Like Disney World."

Andi saw the look of adoration in her daughter's eyes and marveled at the feelings rocketing through her.

A year ago she had felt condemned to a life of sadness and loneliness. And now, in the space of a few short weeks, her life had been forever changed.

And all because of this tough loner with the heart of gold, who had managed to win her over completely.

With a laugh she brushed her lips over his and felt the familiar rush of heat. "I think it's a wonderful idea, Donovan."

At that his mother blew a kiss while his sister, Bren, wiped a tear from her eyes. Kieran gave his grandson a thumbs-up, and his brothers were both grinning and nudging each other.

Andi tucked her hand in his and gave him a look of blinding love. "Let's go home, Donovan."

Home.

He looked around and realized that home wasn't a place but a feeling. After a lifetime of wandering the world in search of his, he had found it right here. In these children's eyes. In this woman's touch. And finally, at long last, within his own mended heart.

* * * * *

Look for BANNING'S WOMAN,
Book Three in
THE LASSITER LAW *series,*
coming in March 2002 from
Silhouette Intimate Moments.

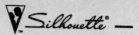

If you enjoyed what you just read,
then we've got an offer you can't resist!

Take 2 bestselling love stories FREE!

Plus get a FREE surprise gift!

Silhouette®

INTIMATE MOMENTS™

In February 2002

MERLINE LOVELACE

brings back
the men—and women—of

CODE NAME: DANGER

Beginning with
HOT AS ICE, IM #1129
He was frozen in time! And she was
just the woman to thaw him out....

Follow the adventures and loves of the
members of the Omega Agency.
Because love is a risky business.

Also look for

DANGEROUS TO HOLD in February 2002
DANGEROUS TO KNOW in July 2002

to see where **CODE NAME: DANGER** began

Available at your favorite retail outlet.

Silhouette®

Where love comes alive™

SIMCD02

CRIMES OF

Passion

Sometimes Cupid's aim can be deadly.

This Valentine's Day, Worldwide Mystery brings you
four stories of passionate betrayal and deadly crime
in one gripping anthology.

Crimes of Passion features FIRE AND ICE,
NIGHT FLAMES, ST. VALENTINE'S DIAMOND,
and THE LOVEBIRDS by favorite romance authors
Maggie Price and B.J. Daniels,
and top mystery authors Nancy Means Wright
and Jonathan Harrington.

Where red isn't just for roses.

Available January 2002 at your favorite retail outlet.

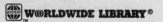 **WORLDWIDE LIBRARY** ®

WCOP

Silhouette

INTIMATE MOMENTS™

LONE STAR
LCC
COUNTRY
CLUB
EST. 1923

Where Texas society reigns supreme—and appearances are everything!

When a bomb rips through the historic
Lone Star Country Club, a mystery
begins in Mission Creek....

Available February 2002
ONCE A FATHER (IM #1132)
by Marie Ferrarella
A lonely firefighter and a warmhearted doctor fall in love while
trying to help a five-year-old boy orphaned by the bombing.

Available March 2002
IN THE LINE OF FIRE (IM #1138)
by Beverly Bird
Can a lady cop on the bombing task force and a sexy ex-con stop
fighting long enough to realize they're crazy about each other?

Available April 2002
MOMENT OF TRUTH (IM #1143)
by Maggie Price
A bomb tech returns home to Mission Creek and discovers that an
old flame has been keeping a secret from him....

And be sure not to miss the Silhouette anthology

Lone Star Country Club: The Debutantes

Available in May 2002

Available at your favorite retail outlet.

Silhouette®
Where love comes alive™

Visit Silhouette at www.eHarlequin.com   SIMLCC